ALIEN TYRANT

Fated Mates of the Sea Sand Warlords
Book One
By Ursa Dax

NOTICES

All rights reserved. No part of this book may be copied, used, transmitted, or shared via any means without express authorization from the author, except for small passages and quotations used for review and marketing purposes.

This is a work of fiction. All characters, events, and incidents in this novel are fictitious and not to be construed as reality or fact.

Alien Tyrant Copyright © 2021 Veronica Doran

ACKNOWLEDGEMENTS

To my husband, RSH, I thank you for your endless support, patience, and cheerleading. To my mother, SMD, who proudly reads everything I produce, no matter how strange and steamy, thank you for your constant enthusiasm for my work and your proofreading skills. And to all my new readers, fans, and friends, thank you so much for entering this new alien world with me. Your kind words, glowing reviews, and excitement for these characters truly makes everything worth it!

- Ursa

TRIGGER WARNINGS

Contains on-page battle scenes and violence. Death of family members (parents and grandmother) mentioned in the heroine's backstory. Abduction-by-the-hero trope, as well as abduction in general by other parties. Alien/non-human hero.

PROLOGUE
Buroudei

It was deep in the night when I heard the sound. Whisper soft and high-pitched, trilling in the darkness. A sound a warrior only hears once in his lifetime. A sound that cannot be ignored.

The Lavrika.

It had finally come.

I rose from my bed of dakrival hides, padding over the sand then lifting the flap of my tent, staring out into the night, over the endless sea of sand. Above me, our many cracked and broken moons glowed in a long line, stretching from horizon to horizon in a shattered band.

The sound trilled again, low, half a whistle, half a warble, and instinctively I crouched, stilling myself, placing my claws to the ground. I let out a long, steadying breath, relaxing, letting my eyes swing back and forth until finally, I saw it. The Lavrika, moving smoothly towards me from a great distance, getting closer every moment.

I had only heard it described before now. Men much luckier than me, lucky to have been called by the Lavrika to learn who fate had chosen as their mates, had told me stories of it. Of its long, starlight body, slipping through the sand like a ghost. And now I was among those lucky ones. One of the warriors the Lavrika had come to.

After all this time.

The descriptions I'd heard fell short. Even now, upon viewing the sacred creature as it reached me, I was hard-pressed to find the words to describe it. Its body, long and winding, shimmered, half-here and half-not. I could see the sand, turned deep silvery-black in the moonlit darkness, through its skin. I was one of the tallest of my tribe, and the Lavrika was easily as long as four or five of me laid end to end. It was truly magnificent. My chest clenched at the sight.

It swung its great head, rising from the sand. It had no legs or arms that I could see, but was able to raise its head high off the ground using only the strength of its silvery spine, a structure I saw pulsing beneath its translucent skin. It fixed me with shifting eyes that glowed brighter than any star, and I rose slowly, my tail jerking unintentionally as I did so. I could not help it. My heart was pounding in my chest. I was going to learn of my mate. I was finally going to find out what destiny would make of me. Whom I would bind myself with, always. Whom I would raise cubs with. The future Gahnala of our tribe.

The Lavrika dipped its head, then turned with perfect, curving grace, its long body slithering away from me the way it had come. Quickly, I dressed, putting on my simple hide loincloth, then strapping my ablik knives, long and deadly sharp, to my back. At the last moment, I grabbed my axe, also carved from ablik stone, hefting it in one hand and grasping my spear in the other. I had no need of weapons where the peaceful Lavrika was concerned, gigantic though it was. But there were other creatures out there, in the sand. Ones with far worse tidings for me than the Lavrika.

I stepped out of my tent, letting the flap fall closed. For a brief moment, I wondered if I should wake my right hand man, my closest commander, Galok. But as I watched the Lavrika wind further from me, I decided against it. I would be back by tomorrow. This path was to be walked alone.

And so I left behind the tents of my people and forged forward, every step taking me closer and closer to my future.

I followed the Lavrika for some time. I already knew where it would lead me. Everyone in my tribe, and all the other tribes of the Sea

Sands, knew where to find the Lavrika Pools, tucked into the caves of the Cliffs of Uruzai. But it was useless to travel there without an invitation from the Lavrika. Only the Lavrika's presence meant that you would see your mate in the pools. A thrill flooded through me as I thought about what was coming, my hands tightening on my axe and spear as I followed the Lavrika's winding tail.

Who will it be? There were not so many women left among us now. Perhaps Zanixia. I had lain with her before. There was much amicable respect between us, though nothing that hinted at a sacred mate bond. Nothing of the all-encompassing, soul-crushing wave of brutal love I'd heard mated men speak of. But the Lavrika Pools could change all that. Warriors saw their fate in those pools, those who were called. And once they saw it, everything changed. I tried to imagine my feelings for Zanixia growing that fiercely, changing so completely. Tried to imagine her not just sharing my bed but ruling the tribe at my side, bearing my children. It was a pleasant enough thought, but it inspired no real fire in my belly. At least, not yet.

I will have to let the Lavrika lead the way. Fantasizing and imagining would do me no good now. I'd already been doing it my entire adult life.

Eventually, a jagged black line became visible on the dark horizon. We were nearing the Cliffs of Uruzai. The Lavrika continued its steady path, and I trod silently behind it, my tail swishing long strokes through the sand. The cliffs grew and grew until finally, after what felt like endless walking, they loomed, huge and imposing, before us. I craned my neck back – it was difficult to see the tops of the cliffs in the darkness. They seemed to jut up and then melt right into the sky.

The Lavrika was slithering along the line of the cliffs, and I hastily followed, suddenly worried that I may lose sight of it now that we were so close. So close to the pools. So close to my fate.

The Lavrika paused, then turned, seeming to disappear into the cliff wall itself. But I knew that it had reached the opening in the stone wall that led to the pools. Hefting my weapons, I jogged after it, coming to a stop at the craggy opening.

A Lavrikala, one of the sacred protectors of the Lavrika and its pools, stood tall, spear in hand. She watched the Lavrika disappear into the cliff, then turned to me, her eyes appraising. I did not recognize her. She was not from my tribe, but was of one of the other Sea Sand clans. She was old, past her mating years, but she stood nearly as tall as me, and gripped her staff with a powerful ease. I raised my tail, winding it around my front and bringing the black tip up to cover my eyes. The gesture was sign of immense respect I gave only to the likes of the Lavrikala now. As a Gahn, a warlord and the leader of my tribe, I had not done such a thing for anyone else since childhood. Usually it was others shielding their eyes from me.

"You may enter, Gahn Buroudei."

My tail relaxed, falling into place behind me. I nodded to the Lavrikala, not bothering to wonder how she knew my name, then moved to follow the Lavrika into the darkness of the cliffside. But then, she spoke again, seemingly more to herself than me, and I halted.

"I should have known the Lavrika would bring a mighty Gahn tonight. This is no ordinary calling to destiny. The air feels... strange."

I stared at her, but she said nothing more, her gaze locked out on the dark sands.

I shook myself, then finally followed the Lavrika to my fate.

It was too dark to see anything at first. I had to feel my way along the inner stone wall of the cliff, moving ever forward. There was no other choice. The passage was narrow, and there was only one way to go. After a few cramped moments of darkness, a faint glow ahead became visible, and the passage began to widen, eventually expanding out into a large, wide cave. It was cooler in here than it had been outside, and humid, too. The sensation was strange on my skin. I was used to the blistering dry heat of the desert during day time. This moisture was completely foreign to me. Though I knew where the Lavrika Pools were, I had never actually entered the caves before.

I let my eyes adjust to the light, taking it all in. The cave was large, its floor dotted with milky bodies of glowing liquid, and at the other end I could see other openings that led to deeper caves. But it did not seem we would need to go deeper into the cliff. The Lavrika had stopped here, its long body curled and waiting, watching me.

It waited at the edge of the largest pool, its body glowing with the same white iridescence as the liquid in the pools, the only light in the dim place. We called the liquid Lavrika's blood. It had many properties, not the least of which was a remarkable healing ability. But on a night like tonight, when the Lavrika led you here, it would show you your future.

My heart pounded, my jaw clenching so hard it felt like my very fangs would crack. Wordlessly, I removed my weapons and my loincloth. I had heard tell from the others that you were to enter the pool pure and naked as a cub. And now that I was here, it felt only right and natural to do just that.

I moved ahead, the claws on my feet clicking against the dark stone floor. The Lavrika watched me for one more moment, then it slipped into the pool, hardly creating a ripple.

It's time.

Why did I feel like I was about to charge into the greatest battle of my life?

I stepped forward, plunging one foot into the Lavrika's blood, then another. The incline was gradual, and I moved slowly forward, the liquid reaching to my thighs, then my groin, then my waist. Everywhere the Lavrika's blood touched thrummed with intense, surging energy. I had no idea where the Lavrika was now. The liquid was milky and thick, making it impossible to see.

How deep do I go?

I stopped when the liquid was chest-high, glancing around the place, unsure what to do next.

When in doubt, follow the Lavrika.

The thought pounded through me and, without another moment's hesitation, I plunged forward, submerging myself completely.

The sensation was so overpowering that I shut my eyes against it, instinctively raising my arms, as if to fight off a terrible enemy. *A Gahn should never close his eyes or hide from any power. Face this, Buroudei. Face this, now.* I wrenched my eyes open, allowing my hands to move through the thick liquid to my sides, though it barely felt like liquid, now. Not wet, not hindering my breathing at all. I was floating, floating in a vast emptiness of white, so bright and blinding I felt like a krixel had taken me in its claws and flown me face-first into the nearest star. My chest tightened. Every muscle, every limb, was primed and ready. Ready for whatever may be coming.

At least, that's what I thought. But nothing could have prepared me for the face that materialized in the Lavrika's blood.

It was unlike any face I had ever seen before. It was not Zanixia, nor anyone from my clan or even from my people at all. Where our people's brows were dark and heavy, hers were almost non-existent, tiny strokes across her face. Where our noses were largely flat, hers had a strange, slim, raised bridge to it. Where our skin was deep-coloured, like the Sea Sands of Zaphrinax, hers was pale, almost as pale as the Lavrika's blood around me. As more of her came into my shifting view, I saw her hands – as pale as her face, and basically clawless. Her ears were soft, round, and low, mostly hidden by long, light hair. She wore strange garb, and, from what I could see, had no tail.

Despite her strangeness, a new longing pulsed through me, lighting up every part of my body. I fought through the thick liquid, fought to move closer to her, to grasp one of her strange little hands, to ask her where on Zaphrinax she came from. I couldn't stop looking at her eyes, eyes a colour I had never seen before. White around the edges, the centres round and coloured similarly to valok plants, but lighter and brighter, with a dark point in the middle.

At first, it had seemed that I was viewing her from afar. That I was privy to some kind of secret vision. But then those strange, bright eyes locked onto mine, and her face changed, her slim brows rising, her soft mouth opening, revealing tiny, blunted teeth. Shock burst inside me.

Can you see me? Can you hear me?

My words went nowhere. And before I knew what was happening, she was fading, her features growing indistinct, her body pulling painfully away from mine.

No!

I reached one hand towards her. I couldn't let her go just yet. Not until I knew how I could find her.

But that was not the way of the Lavrika. One did not pull one's mate from the deep. One only got a single glimpse.

She was gone. My tail thrashed, my legs pumping to propel myself deeper into the pool, to catch any last sight of her I could. But then, a powerful grip wound around me, and I was launched from the pool.

I snarled as my back collided hard with the stone wall of the cave and I fell to the floor.

I stood quickly, tail still twitching, facing the pool once more. The Lavrika's head was just above the surface and it watched me silently. I quelled an agonized growl, knowing that it would offer me no more tonight. It would throw me back out of the pool as soon as I approached. If it were another warrior I faced, even another Gahn, I'd tear his head from his body for trying to stop me. But one could not doubt the Lavrika, nor could one oppose it. I had gotten all I would receive.

But all it left me with were questions, one of them rising above all others, pounding inside me like a war drum.

Who are you? Who are you? Who are you?

CHAPTER ONE
Cece

I pulled on a sports bra, a long-sleeved T-shirt, and leggings, fumbling in the dark. The sun hadn't even risen yet, and I was already out of bed for some God-forsaken reason, readying myself for a run. I clenched my jaw, lacing up my shoes then pulling my long, light chestnut hair, tangled from sleep, into a messy bun on the top of my head. I glanced at my phone. *Not even five am. Damn.* I was definitely not what you'd consider to be a morning person.

So then why was I up at this unholy fucking hour, getting ready to drag my body though the streets of Toronto on a cold March morning? *Good question.*

In all honesty, I wasn't quite sure myself. I'd woken, drenched in sweat, from the most vivid dream of my life. Everything had been bright, so bright. So bright I could barely see. So bright I was afraid. But then, suddenly, there had been a hand reaching for me through all that white. And though it had been inhuman and strange, I knew that I was supposed to reach out and take it. But I'd woken up before I could do so, and I'd been struck by a bizarre and unshakable sense of loss. I couldn't stay in bed anymore after that, couldn't even stay in my basement apartment. I had to outrun this feeling. The feeling of grief.

As I locked my apartment's door behind me and started running, I ruminated on the dream. I didn't need a psychoanalyst to tell me what it meant. A feeling of loss, a hand reaching for me, surrounded by white? What other kind of dream could I expect right after losing my grandmother, my last remaining relative on the face of this whole freaking planet?

Shit.

My throat tightened, and I ran faster, pushing my body so hard that I had no time or energy for tears. Grammy may not have left me much – a little money to see me through the rest of my linguistics PhD program at the University of Toronto. But she did leave one giant, old-lady shaped hole, right in the centre of my chest. It had been two weeks since her heart attack, and it was still hard to breathe without her.

Stop.

These thoughts were not helping.

She'd be telling you, right now, to stop the belly-aching and to put your big girl panties on.

After losing her husband decades ago, and her only child, my mother, when I was a baby, she'd dealt with more than her fair share of pain and had come through it stronger than ever. I only hoped I had a fraction of her grit.

I slowed my pace, yanking my phone and earbuds from the pocket of my leggings, shoving the cord into the sound jack and pushing play on one of my Spotify playlists. If I couldn't outrun grief, I could drown it out in the dulcet tones of Lorde and Lady Gaga.

But those earbuds turned out to be my undoing. Lodged firmly in my ears, music pumping, I didn't hear them coming. I didn't stand a fucking chance.

Because before I knew what was happening, I was grabbed from behind, yanked right off my feet, and thrown into the back of a van. It happened so fast I didn't have half a thought in my head of screaming or defending myself. Those instincts kicked in late – far too late. After the doors to the back of the windowless van had been shut behind me and the vehicle started to move.

Oh, fuck no.

This was why Grammy was always harping on me not to listen to music during runs. Because I'd end up in a real-life version of Taken. Only I didn't have a Liam Neeson-esque dad ready to save me. I only had... Well... Me.

After taking a moment to get used to the jostling movement of the van, I quickly sat up, bracing my hands on the floor and swinging my head around the dark space. It was like some kind of cargo van – an empty cube with nothing in it. Nothing but me, anyway. There was almost no light, and my breath came in ragged gasps as I willed my eyes to adjust to the darkness. My heart was about to break right out of my poor ribs, and my hands were slick with sweat. Panic threatened to overwhelm me. *I'm just a PhD student, for God's sake. I am not equipped to handle this.*

But no. No, that wasn't true.

The sudden denial, the flood of strength, didn't come from me. It came from Grammy. She'd always told me I could do anything. That I was smart and worthy and strong. And my Grammy never told a lie.

Think, Cece, think.

My eyes were somewhat adjusted to things, now, though there wasn't much to see. The back of the van was walled off from the driver's compartment, so I couldn't see the motherfuckers who were driving this thing. There was no way to get to them. My only other option was to try to escape. I hadn't been tied up, thankfully. At least, not yet.

Well, that's a grim thought.

The van swerved around a corner, tossing me into the metal side, and my shoulder screamed in pain.

"Oh, come on!" I hissed, trying to breathe through the pain. I steadied myself, holding myself against the wall in case we swerved again, gingerly pressing my fingers against my arm and rotating it.

Not broken. But I'm going to have a hell of a bruise.

Crawling along the floor, I found my way to the back doors of the van, feeling along their metal surface. There didn't seem to be any way to open them from the inside. But there was no way I was going to let that stop me from trying. I had a sinking feeling that I did not want to get to whatever destination was in store for me.

I snorted at myself. I didn't want to find out where the pedo van that I had been tossed into was going to take me? *No shit, Sherlock.*

"Alright," I said out loud to myself, voice shaking. "If I can't open the doors with a handle, I guess I have to try to ram them open somehow."

But the only thing available to ram anything with was my own body.

So the question becomes, do I use my good shoulder and potentially screw up both sides of my body? Or use the already sore one?

Neither option was particularly palatable. But I had to do something. The pain in my left shoulder had faded to a dull throb, and I didn't really want that sensation radiating from both sides of my body.

Messed up shoulder it is, then.

I got shakily to my feet, widening my stance to try to stay stable as we continued driving wherever the hell it was we were going. I took a few clumsy steps back.

Here goes nothing.

I launched forward towards the doors, the side of my body colliding with the metal in a vicious crash. Pain exploded in my shoulder, radiating down my arm, and I collapsed to the floor, my breath half-knocked out me.

Blinking back tears, I was readying myself to stand and try again, and again, to try as many times as it would take, when words echoed somewhere above me, booming in the small space.

"Don't do that," a bored-sounding male voice commanded from what sounded to be right above me.

I flinched, then squinted upwards and finally saw it. A black square in the upper corner of the van. A speaker, and, next to it, what looked to be a small camera. I flipped what I assumed to be the camera the bird, then quickly lowered my hand, thinking better of it. Probably didn't want to piss these guys off any more than was necessary.

"Where are you taking me?" I shouted towards the speaker and camera, trying to will my voice to sound steadier than I felt.

No answer.

"God damn it."

I stood again, cradling my aching arm.

"Tell me where you're taking me. Or I'm going to keep ramming up against that door."

It wasn't a great plan. But it was all I had.

There was still no answer.

Fine. Have it your way.

I turned, despite the screaming of my shoulder, getting ready to launch myself at the door once more, when the van suddenly screeched to a stop, sending me flying to the floor in a heap. Before I could right myself, the doors were yanked open. Instinctively, I crab-crawled backwards, cornering myself against the front wall of the vehicle. A man, dressed all in black, jumped into the van and grabbed me, wrestling me beneath him as I screamed, spat, and kicked.

I'm not going to die in the back of this fucking van. Not today.

I managed to get my knee up, ramming it between the man's legs as hard as I could. He gave a choked-sounding grunt, and I took advantage of the moment of surprise, wriggling out from under him and scrabbling for the open doors. I was so close. So close to being able to jump right out those doors -

- when a hand closed around my ankle, yanking me back. My arms slid out from under me as I was pulled, my chin colliding painfully with the metal floor, rattling my teeth.

"No, no, no," I said, over and over again. It was like that was the only word left in my brain.

A second man appeared at the back of the van, jumping inside.

"Jesus, Hanson, can't even keep a 25-year-old grad student under control?"

"Shut the fuck up and just give her the damn shot," the man holding me growled as I fought to pull my wrists from his iron grip.

Shot? Did one of them have a gun?

The thought renewed my strength and I fought as hard as I could, with everything I had left, my teeth sinking into the first man's forearm.

"Fucking hell, hurry up, man! I'm gonna get tetanus or some shit from this."

"You're fine. All of them have clean medicals. Anyway, I got it. Here we go. Nighty night, Princess."

There was a prick of pain in my neck, then a creeping, liquid burning, spreading under my skin.

And then, there was only darkness.

CHAPTER TWO
Cece

"Y'all think she's OK?"

"How the hell should I know? I don't even know if *we're* OK."

"You know what I mean. She's the only one who hasn't woken up yet. She looks like she got banged up real good."

"Hold up! I feel like I just saw her eyelids move."

"Bullshit."

"I swear! Dude, look! She's totally waking up."

Strange voices swirled around me, their words coming tantalizingly close to being understood in my foggy brain. I was tired. So tired. Everything felt heavy. Even my tongue. And especially my eyelids. There was pain, too. In my arm and my shoulder and my face.

I'm just going to sleep a little more...

"Oh, no you don't."

I was being shaken, now. And the words were coming in more clearly.

"This is no time for nappin', hun. Wake up."

Is that you, Grammy?

I forced my eyelids open, my eyes tracking left and right as I tried to focus in on the face in front of me. It wasn't Grammy. *Of course not. Idiot.*

The face above me was young, maybe even a year or two younger than me, with high cheekbones and almost invisible blond brows, one of which was pierced, set over deep blue eyes. A stud in her nostril glimmered, and she had another piercing in her nose, a ring that hung down low, between her nostrils. In my confusion, I couldn't remember the name of that kind of piercing. All I could conjure up was the image of a bull. I looked closer at her, trying to get my eyes to focus better. Though her features were lovely, delicate, even, her shaved head gave her a take-no-shit appearance, and her stormy expression could rival the anger of any bull on the planet.

"Why isn't she answering? Maybe she hit her head."

Huh? Had someone been asking me a question?

"Give her a minute and let her catch her breath. Dang."

The piercings girl's face got closer.

"Whaaat's youuur naaaaaame?" She said slowly, dragging the syllables out. I heard someone scoff behind her.

My name? That was something I could remember.

"Celia. Cece." My voice cracked. Damn, my mouth was dry.

"Here, give her this."

A hand came into view, passing Piercings Girl a metal bottle which she opened and pressed to my lips.

Um. Should I really be drinking this?

I had no idea where the hell I was, or how I'd gotten there. But I was so, so thirsty.

Screw it.

I took a sip, relieved to find it seemed to be just plain old water. I took another sip before inhaling some and starting to choke, each cough sending shooting pain through my head.

"Quick, get her sittin' up."

Piercings Girl passed the bottle to someone else, then reached around my back, helping to pull me upright. It took a minute for the coughing and the pounding in my head to subside, and when it did, I finally raised my eyes and looked around.

I, we, were in a strange-looking room. The walls were grey, as were the floors, shining like brushed metal. I was sitting on the bottom of what seemed to be a bunk bed. There was another set of bunks directly across from where I sat, and I noticed another girl sitting there, staring at me. Her pale face had a bruise blooming along one side, and when she saw me looking, she shifted her glossy black hair to try to hide it.

"I'm Katerina. Kat for short," the girl with the piercings, who was sitting next to me, said. She had the water bottle back and held it out to me again, and I drank, being careful not to confuse my stomach and my lungs this time. "That's Melanie." She pointed at the dark-haired girl across from me, who nodded stiffly.

"And I'm Theresa," said a voice from beside me. I looked to the side, then up, to meet the gaze of another girl around my age standing next to me, leaning one elbow against the metal frame of the top bunk. Her straw-coloured hair was cut bluntly at her shoulders, and her brown eyes were looking at me kindly. Her yellow sundress looked strangely out of place in the metallic grey of the room. When I looked closer, I noticed one of the straps was ripped and hanging down by her side. As if someone had torn it. As if she'd been in a struggle.

"Here," she said, sitting down on the mattress beside me and reaching for the water bottle.

Wordlessly, I handed it to her, and she poured a little of the liquid into her hand before moving her cupped palm up to my chin. I sucked in a breath and jerked back at the stinging sensation. She dabbed lightly at my skin, then frowned.

"Well, that didn't do a whole heck of a lot, hun. Sorry. Nasty gash you got there." It was only then I noticed the Southern drawl that shaped her voice. *She must be American. An international student?*

But wait. This definitely didn't seem to be the University of Toronto. At least, no building I had ever seen.

"Where are we?" I croaked, gently touching my chin and wincing.

Kat snorted.

"No fucking clue, dude."

Melanie's mouth thinned into a grim line and Theresa shook her head.

"Yeah, none of us know. I was the first one to wake up in this here room. Then some army guys brought in Melanie, then Kat. And then you."

"Army guys?"

What was she talking about? None of this made any sense.

"Yeah. They were wearin' army uniforms of some kind. And they spoke English when they talked to each other. But they didn't say anythin' to us."

"Are we... Are we in the US?"

"Fuck if I know," Kat replied. "I mean, I kind of hope we are. That means we haven't left the country yet."

"Well, I'm from Canada, so I don't know what that tells us," I said with a harsh sigh.

Kat's pale brows shot up.

"Seriously? Shit. Well, I have no clue then. The three of us are American."

"Do you know how we got here?"

There was a series of memories flickering at the edge of my brain. I was doing everything I could to latch onto them, but they kept fluttering away.

"I woke up the soonest, and so far I remember the most," Theresa said. "But even that ain't a whole lot. I remember I was walkin' home from my boyfriend's. Well, ex-boyfriend's. I'd just dumped his cheatin' ass. It was late and dark, and then someone grabbed me and tossed me into a truck or a van or somethin'. Then I woke up here. And that's all I got."

A van.

That was just enough to click things into place. I stared down at my outfit. *Running clothes.*

"Yeah, I think I was out for a run. Someone grabbed me..."

Melanie nodded from across the small space.

"Yup. It's the same story for all of us. From what we can remember. We think we were drugged."

"Well, that would explain the memory loss and headache," I muttered, rubbing my fingertips against my temples in small circles. I knew I should be thinking, trying to come up with a plan, trying to do *something*. But I just couldn't. It was like my brain and body had just totally given up.

"Anyway, that basically brings you up to speed. You know what we know," Kat said, scooting her hips forward then flopping back on the mattress, arms akimbo.

It didn't feel like I had been brought up to any kind of speed. At all. It felt like I was at a total standstill.

A sudden sound at the door at the far end of the small room made us all jump. Kat immediately shimmied upright, and Theresa and Melanie both stood. I followed suit, the four of us turning to face the door as it swung inward.

"Oh good. You're all awake."

A woman with ginger hair pulled into a tight bun strolled into the room. Like Theresa had said, she was wearing a camo military uniform, with words embroidered on either side of her chest. On the left, in black thread, it said, "Chapman." On the right, "US Army."

"Everyone's waiting in the mess hall. You're the last group. Let's go."

"Go where?" I said shakily, already inching away from her. Theresa grabbed my hand and squeezed.

The red-haired soldier looked at me flatly, like I was half brain dead.

"We're going to the mess hall," she said slowly, as if I were too dumb to understand.

Kat exploded from beside me, saying all the words that were flying through my own head.

"Fuck you. You what what she meant. *What* mess hall? Where the fuck are we?"

She didn't reply, but instead turned on her heel, her tan boots squeaking against the smooth floor, and stepped out into the hallway.

The four of us looked at each other.

"I don't think we have a choice," said Melanie. Kat looked like she was about to fight a bitch, but Theresa nodded solemnly.

"At the very least maybe we'll get some information," I said. It was decided. I was going to go out there and see what the hell was up, even if Kat or the others didn't want to.

I stepped forward, towards the door, and the other three girls followed.

Out in the hallway Chapman stood with two other soldiers, both men.

"Let's go," she said, walking ahead of us.

The two men positioned themselves behind us, caging us into our formation, and we started to walk down a long hallway. The floor and walls were of the same brushed metal as our room, with subtle glowing lights built into the arched ceiling. The hallway seemed to be curving, like we were following it around the outside of a massive oval.

"Feels like we're in goddamn Star Trek," Kat muttered.

Chapman glanced back, her expression a warning, but Kat met her gaze head on.

"Honestly, yeah," I said, subtly glancing around. This place was like nothing I'd ever seen. All smooth edges, blinking lights, and shining chrome.

Eventually we were led through a large, open door and into something that seemed a little more familiar. The mess hall, as Chapman had called it, looked a lot like the cafeterias I was used to at school. Only instead of large windows and wood and plastic and bright lights, everything was made from the same silvery surface, and the light was low, with no windows. At one end of the room, a long row of counters, the kind you'd see at a buffet or in a cafeteria, stood empty.

Guess it's not chow time. My stomach rolled nauseously at the thought of any kind of food.

"Here," Chapman said, leading the four of us to sit at the closest table. We did so, looking around. The large room's other tables were also occupied. My heart sank as I saw all the people, all the young women, in the exact same situation as us. Looking confused, angry, scared, some of them with torn clothing, bruises, and cuts.

This is not good. The fact that we were all young women was leading me more and more to the conclusion that we were in some bizarro sex trafficking ring. My hands curled tightly on the edge of the table, and I saw Kat, Theresa, and Melanie's faces darken with thoughts just like mine.

But when a tall, broad shouldered man with silver hair, also wearing a US military uniform, strolled to the front of the room, my confusion only deepened.

"Why the fuck is the army here?" Kat hissed quietly from beside me.

Melanie's dark eyes tracked the man's movements. "Maybe they're in costume or pretending. Maybe it's some kind of setup."

"OK, but look at this place," I whispered, and we all cast furtive glances around the room. "This doesn't seem like your average criminal enterprise. It's not like we woke up in a warehouse somewhere." The more I thought about the insanity of the situation, the less and less everything made sense. If this was a legitimate military operation of some kind, with the budget needed to create a building like this, why the hell were we kidnapped off the streets and drugged?

There were similar whispered conversations happening at the tables all around us, and the man at the front called out.

"Hello, everyone. I'm Colonel Anthony Jackson."

"Colonel, that's high up, right?" I asked, and Theresa nodded from across the table.

"I'm sure you're all wondering why you've been brought here."

Kat snorted, and a girl from somewhere in the room yelled out, "You mean abducted?"

Colonel Jackson didn't even flinch. He ignored the girl who yelled and continued smoothly, his eyes grey and flat. A shiver ran through me.

"You have all been specially selected to serve your planet on a confidential mission. This mission is one of the first of its kind, and its secrecy is of the utmost importance. Thus, you were selected and taken before any information could be leaked."

"Yo, what the *actual fuck* are you talking about?" Kat shouted, standing. Colonel Jackson eyed her, then shifted his gaze somewhere behind her, nodding once. Chapman stepped forward and clocked Kat on the back of the head with the butt of what looked to be a pistol.

"Oh my God," I stammered, barely catching her as she fell with a yelp. She crumpled back into her seat beside me, rubbing her shaved head, which I could see was already swelling where she'd been hit. "Are you OK?"

"What do you think?" She replied, staring viciously at Chapman, then back at the Colonel. But he ignored her, as if she were a fly that had been squashed and was no longer buzzing annoyingly nearby.

"As I was saying, this mission is of the utmost secrecy. You have all been selected for your areas of expertise – chemistry, biology, anthropology, botany, linguistics." My throat tightened at the mention of my PhD program. So it wasn't some insane mistake that I'd been brought here.

"I don't have any expertise! I'm just a student. Please, I want to go home." The voice was a quiet and trembling one, coming from a girl I couldn't see well on the other side of the room.

"I'm happy to say that if our mission is successful, you will all be allowed to go home," Colonel Jackson replied, his voice devoid of emotion.

"Allowed?!" An angry voice piped up. "What do you mean, *allowed*? I'm an American citizen, I have rights." Several heads nodded, and murmurs of agreement rippled through the crowd. It emboldened me, and I raised my voice.

"And what about me? I'm not even American! You kidnapped a Canadian citizen!"

Someone else shouted, "*Moi aussi*, I'm from France!"

The Colonel took a breath and closed his eyes for a moment, as if dealing with a bunch of irritating children. His expression filled me with rage. For him, apparently, this was just another annoying day on the job. But to us, it was our whole life, hanging in whatever fucked-up balance he had orchestrated.

After a moment, when most of the talking and questions had died down again, he spoke.

"While this particular mission is largely US military-run, rest assured the program at large is a global effort. The governments from every country represented in this room have sanctioned the mission and our actions."

The breath rushed out of me, leaving me deflated and shaken. *My own government was OK with this? They offered me up like some kind of lamb to slaughter?*

But was it slaughter? Maybe the fact that this appeared to be some kind of legitimate, massively funded military operation meant that we weren't about to disappear off the face of the earth, murdered and thrown in a ditch somewhere...

Another voice piped up, and I realized with a jerk that it was Melanie. Quiet Melanie from our table. Her eyes were hard, her voice steady.

"You said we get to go home if this mission is successful. What is it exactly that you want us to do?"

There was a cold determination in her eyes that I admired. I gulped, trying to fortify myself with some of whatever she had. Theresa sat up straighter at the question, and Kat stopped rubbing the back of her head, leaning forward. I licked my lips, mouth suddenly incredibly dry.

"Unbeknownst to the public, Earth has a large space program, much more advanced than what you see on TV with rockets and moon-landings. We have been searching for energy and materials to sustain life on Earth, and have been also searching for planets to eventually host human colonies."

A collective gasp ran through the crowd, and Colonel Jackson raised his hand for silence, continuing.

"We have discovered numerous new energy sources and resources we need to study further. One of these is a compound we have called IX189, on a planet we have called P14256ABX."

"That isn't, like, Mars or something, right?" I said, stomach sinking. Were we going to be flung out of our entire galaxy? *I've never even been outside of North America.*

"This planet exists in a small galaxy we have named the Ophis Cluster."

"Ophis... That sounds like the Greek word for serpent," I whispered. My thoughts were confirmed when suddenly the blank silver wall behind the colonel lit up, an image being projected on its smooth surface. A hushed silence fell over the room as we stared at a star system none of us had ever seen before, the planets and glittering spray of stars swirling, snakelike, across the screen. The image suddenly shifted, showing a large brownish-looking planet with a ring of what looked to be asteroid chunks, or some other kind of space rocks, surrounding it like the rings of Saturn.

"This is P14256ABX. Our radar technology has picked up a massive energy source on this planet, the compound we have labelled

IX189. The problem is that we can't just go down and get it. This planet is inhabited by a primitive, warlike species that we have yet to establish contact with. We have not yet been down to the surface of the planet, but have orbited it for some time, collecting data. Now that we've collected enough data, our orbiting vessel has left to move on to other projects, and our mission can begin."

Another image flashed on the screen, this one blurry and difficult to make out. I realized with a small cry it was a photo of one of the planet's inhabitants, an honest-to-goodness real life alien. Another round of gasps ran through the room, and someone burst into tears.

Holy fucking fuck. I'd always assumed that with a universe as wide and unknown as ours that there would be life out there somewhere. I just never thought that I'd get a chance to come face to face with it, even as a grainy photo like this.

"For fuck's sake," Kat said, squinting and leaning forward as far as she could across the table. "Is this some conspiracy UFO type shit? They couldn't get a better photo?"

She wasn't wrong. The photo looked like one of the Loch Ness Monster, or Big Foot. I couldn't make out any distinct features on the creature at all, only that it seemed to be bipedal, standing tall on two legs. Or was it three? Before I could look closer, the image vanished, replaced with an image of desert.

"From what we've gathered the atmosphere on the planet is similar to our own, with slightly less oxygen. Similar to high altitude climates on Earth. It shouldn't cause too much of a problem for any of you unless you're vigorously exercising. We've examined your medical records and you all should be fit for such an environment."

Hold the phone. Why did it matter to us what the atmosphere was like? Why did we need to know about the aliens down there? Unless they were planning to…

"Oh my God," Theresa said, her face going pale under her tan. "They're gonna drop us down there. They're literally gonna drop us on the surface of an alien planet."

"No, no way," I shot back quickly, goosebumps breaking out over my skin. That made no sense. At all. "I'm a PhD candidate in the linguistics department. Don't you need tons of training to become an astronaut?"

Theresa's voice fell to a broken whisper.

"Honey, I'm a vet tech. I sure as hell shouldn't be here."

Kat shook her head, and then Melanie turned her dark eyes on us, her face looking resigned.

"Linguistics PhD sounds an awful lot like someone to be an alien translator. And vet tech – well, someone to make conclusions about the local wildlife, I guess? Didn't he say there's a botanist around here somewhere?"

"Um, no," I interjected. "My area of research is translation in pop culture, specifically the creation of subtitles for popular films and TV shows. I literally watch anime for research. That's going to do fuck-all on an alien planet. I assure you."

Melanie just shrugged and turned back to the front of the room. *Yeah, yeah, I get it, you don't make the rules.* As much as I didn't want to admit it, it seemed more and more likely that she was right.

The screen at the front had darkened back to a blank metal slate. I blinked at it, unbelieving. *That's it? That's all we're gonna get?*

"It will take approximately two weeks to reach P14256ABX. During that time, you will receive more thorough instructions on the mission and your duties."

"Our duties?" Kat snarled, jumping up again. Chapman stepped towards her, but Colonel Jackson held up a hand. "My only duty is to get away from you and this whole clusterfuck."

I stood, too, in solidarity, as did Theresa and Melanie. No way was I going to get sucked into some interstellar alien translation job without my consent. I had school to think about, students, a life to get back to. Others were standing now, grumbling, their voices getting louder. Kat continued, grinning at the sight of all the angry women getting out of their chairs.

"See? We don't want to and you can't make us. You may have been able to toss us into vans and get us here, but there's no fucking way you're getting us off this planet."

Colonel Jackson's face remained impassive. The entire room was standing now, waiting for him to make a move. He said nothing, instead pulling a small black object out of his pocket and aiming at the wall that had been a screen a moment before. He pushed a button, and the entire wall seemed to disappear, shimmering out of existence right before our eyes. And what we saw sent me falling back into my chair with a strangled huff, my chest tightening as my knees gave out.

It was earth. The size of a marble, and getting smaller every second, swallowed up by black on all sides as it got further away. No. As *we* got further away. Kat's mouth fell open, and more girls started to cry.

"I'm afraid, Katerina," the Colonel said, his voice like ice, "that that ship has already sailed."

AS SOON AS THE PRESENTATION ended, we were all trundled back into our rooms, escorted by soldiers every step of the way. Although at that point, none of us had much fight left, even Kat. After seeing our planet, the only thing we'd ever known disappear before our eyes... Well... It had kind of stopped any chance of escape in its tracks.

Theresa and Kat climbed the ladders to the top bunks, and Melanie and I collapsed into the bottom ones. There was silence for a moment, as we all contemplated just what on Earth – or what in wherever we were now – was going on. But it wasn't long before Kat spoke up, her voice dripping with venom.

"I don't buy this for a fucking second."

"Don't buy what? You think they're lyin'? You think we're still on Earth somewhere?" The note of hope in Theresa's voice from the bunk above me almost broke my heart.

"No, I think that part is real," Melanie interjected, and I nodded. Every instinct was telling me that we were no longer anywhere close to home.

"No, yeah, I get that. Bye bye, big blue planet. See you never," Kat said. "I just don't believe for a second that A, this mission is actually legit, and B, that they're going to let us go home afterwards."

I gritted my teeth against an onslaught of threatening tears.

"Don't say that," I managed to choke out.

"Sorry, dude, but I think it's true. Think about it. This mission is so top secret that they literally had to kidnap us and drug us to get us here, you think they're going to just let us waltz back into our lives afterwards? And what about the fact that we're all women, huh? And the fact that we're all young or students and definitely not the kind of experts you'd want on a mission like this? Why aren't they sending the *crème de la crème*, top notch scientists and shit, to deal with this?"

I pressed the palms of my hands to my burning eyes. I had no answers for her.

But Melanie did.

"They're not sending the best they have because they think we're going to die." Her words crashed through the air, heavy as stone. "They're hoping that, if by some miracle, we can do something for them, then at least we have some knowledge that may be useful. But they're not going to send their best scientists on a suicide mission." Her voice fell, hard and low. "And the fact that we're all women, well... I bet they're hoping that if we don't get murdered on sight, then maybe we'll just get raped instead."

"Oh my God, no, Melanie," I said, sitting up and looking at her. She was laying still, staring up at the underside of Kat's bunk. Her voice was a whisper when she spoke again.

"I don't know about you guys, but if I don't come back, if I disappear, there's no one who would look for me."

Kat sighed from above her.

"Girl, same. My mom's an addict who I haven't seen in years and my dad's in jail."

Theresa groaned. "Oh my God. Shit. Same. I grew up in the foster care system and I just moved to a new town and dumped my boyfriend, literally the only person who knows me there."

Panic swelled inside me. No way, this couldn't be true. I wasn't like that, was I? Someone who could disappear and barely leave a trace? Somebody no one would miss? I had Grammy! *Had Grammy. Past tense.* But what about my PhD supervisor, Dr MacLaren? He would file a police report, for sure. But then again... What if my whole university was in on whatever this was?

My throat tightened painfully, and I bit down on my lips so hard I tasted blood. They were right. They were absolutely right. We were nobodies on Earth, and we were about to be nobodies who died on a faraway planet.

Hell no.

Everything in my body rebelled against that possibility. I got up, pacing the room, the other girls watching me.

"OK, maybe you're right. You probably are. But I sure as hell do not plan to die in the middle of another galaxy."

Kat sat up, her eyes burning with blue fire.

"What do you have in mind? I'm all for some mutiny."

I laughed, a short, humourless bark.

"They've got armed soldiers every few metres in this place. I don't think we stand a chance with something like that."

"So?" Kat said. "At least we'll go out in a blaze of glory. Go out on our terms."

"Look, if we try something like that, we're basically guaranteed to die. Melanie already outlined why we're expendable. But what if we do everything we can to learn in the next few weeks, do everything we can to ensure our survival down there? He said we can breathe the atmosphere. Maybe we could escape and survive somehow."

"And," Theresa added, that heart-breaking note of hope back in her voice, "maybe the aliens will be friendly."

Kat burst out laughing.

"You're nuts! Did you see the thing in that photo? It's not gonna be like some golden retriever at your vet's office."

"We don't know that. We don't know anythin' about them. We do know whoever's runnin' this brought a linguist." Theresa looked at me over the edge of her bunk. "So they must have reason to think the aliens have language, some kind of intelligence. Maybe we can communicate with them."

"Yeah, that'll go over well. 'Hey, aliens. Please don't try to fuck or murder us. By the way, will you give our military all the special energy juice your planet's running on?'"

"OK, well, I don't know," Theresa responded with a huff, flopping back onto her bunk. "But Cece's right. A mutiny will get us shot instantly. Honestly, I'd rather take my chances on the planet."

"Shot by my own people or eaten by an alien. Who the fuck cares. Whatever," Kat mumbled, lying down again. Melanie rolled over, facing the wall.

"Look, we don't have to figure all of this out now," I said, slowly lowering myself to my bunk. "But let's just promise each other that we'll do our best to get out of this alive somehow. That we pay attention, learn everything we can over the next couple of weeks, and give this thing the best shot we have."

"I will," Theresa said instantly from above me.

"Fine," Kat said.

Melanie said nothing, but I saw a small nod of her head.

I swallowed, nodding to myself. *Well, that's something at least.* I laid back in my bunk, trying to ignore the intense pressure building in my chest. Theresa's words repeated over and over in my head. *Maybe we can communicate with them...* Damn. If anyone was going to have a hope of making friends with our new alien buddies, it was going to be me.

And, so help me God, if that didn't light the hottest fucking fire under my ass.

CHAPTER THREE
Cece

The next two weeks passed in a fevered blur of eating, sleeping, and trying to decode the language of the planet we were rapidly approaching. After breakfast each day, we were all separated to different training rooms. Mine was a tiny dark office with a single computer and a set of headphones which played snippets of the alien language we'd recorded from our orbiting research vessel. The audio recordings, alongside very grainy photos and videos, had already been analyzed by Earth linguists way above my pay grade, but even they hadn't been able to make much of it. So far, we had a list of nouns we were mostly sure about, based on where the aliens seemed to be and what they were doing in the accompanying videos and photos. Otherwise, the language was completely without context or clues. I listened, day after day, to the same static-filled recordings, trying to gain some greater kind of understanding of what we were about to plunge into. The aliens must have had fairly humanoid mouths, as I could sort of replicate the sounds, though with some difficulty. The sounds of their language were guttural, many of the consonants clicking at the back of the throat. And their voices were deep and booming. The first time I'd put my headphones in and pressed play, my heart had thrummed in my chest, my skin pricking with goosebumps, to hear such a strange, deep voice, a voice from across the universe, growling in my ears.

When the other girls and I crashed into bed for lights out each night, I remained awake, going over and over the few words I knew, trying to untangle the mess of the rest of the language. Long after the others had gone to sleep, I tossed and turned, anxiety building every day that we got closer to the planet and that I hadn't made some kind of linguistic breakthrough. Our survival could come down to me and my communications skills. I had to do better. I had to do *something*.

But the two weeks came to their end, and I'd made very little headway other than identifying what seemed to be a few more nouns the other linguists had missed. Ablik, as far as I could tell, seemed to mean weapon. Or maybe stick. Or shovel. Valok was something on the ground that the aliens looked like they picked up and stabbed, then ate. Maybe a small animal that they sucked the blood and guts out of. *Gross.* I had about fifty other nouns stored in the back of brain, words I'd memorized with anxious intensity, repeating them over and over as I walked the halls, as I showered, as I ate the crappy space ship food, even as I peed. But that was it. That's all I had. A handful of nouns to try to negotiate with an alien race. *No pressure.*

Panic churned in my guts as we rose on that final day, knowing today was the day we'd descend to the surface. Everyone else seemed to feel as I did, and Kat, Theresa, Melanie, and I got dressed silently, shrugging into the plain grey uniforms we'd been given not long after arriving on the ship. Over the lightweight grey track pants and grey tank tops, we put on our solar protection jackets – pale tan in colour, with long sleeves and a hood with an attached visor. We'd been given packs, too, with supplies: rations; water bottles; first aid kits; and futuristic, too-powerful-for-over-the-counter sunscreens that went on thick and blue on our skin.

Chapman and a couple of other soldiers, all wearing solar protection jackets over their uniforms, showed up at our door a few moments after we'd gotten dressed.

"Time to go," she said, her face blank.

The four of us looked at each other, saying nothing. Because really, what was there to say? *Good luck everyone, don't die.*

The four of us were led through the long curving hall to a part of the ship we'd never been in, coming to a stop before a large set of round, metal doors. Chapman yanked some kind of badge from her pocket and tapped it against a small screen beside the doors, causing them to to slide open smoothly.

"Welcome to the bridge," she said, gesturing us inside.

"Whoa," Theresa whispered, and Kat whistled, breaking the stoic silence of our little group.

I sucked in a breath. *Whoa indeed.*

We'd gotten used to the spaceship over the past couple of weeks, and it no longer felt foreign to us. But this? This was something straight out of a science fiction movie set. The bridge was large, curving, with at least twelve different seats and console areas set up, where military pilots and technicians were typing and working with singular focus. Colonel Jackson stood at the front, his hands tucked neatly behind his back, and behind him was a massive open view screen, a gargantuan windshield that yielded us our first glimpse of the planet.

The photos we'd seen did nothing to convey the reality of what we saw now. There was a savage sort of beauty to the planet, its surface a deep, coppery gold, the asteroid belt encircling it like a brutal studded belt.

"I didn't know we were already so close," I said, my voice tight. I wasn't ready. We weren't ready. *This can't be actually happening.*

"Good, everyone's here and equipped with their packs." Colonel Jackson nodded approvingly as Kat, Theresa, Melanie, and I stepped forward to join the rest of the women already present on the bridge.

"It will take us about fifteen minutes to descend to the planet's surface."

Holy shit. Fifteen minutes? Fifteen minutes until we potentially get blasted off the face of this fucking world? Great.

"Don't we need to, like, strap in or something?" Someone asked from nearby, but Colonel Jackson shook his head.

"No, our tech is much more advanced than what you've seen in the movies. It should be a pretty smooth ride, but I will direct you all to sit against the back wall of the room in case it gets a little bumpy."

My hands shaking, I took off my backpack and sat against the wall, gripping the grey fabric of the bag between my legs. Theresa gave me a wan smile, her face tinted pale blue from the sunscreen we'd put on.

Colonel Jackson remained standing at the front.

"Now, as we've already outlined, when we get to the planet's surface, we will remain at the vessel until the natives come to us. Based on how territorial they are, and how in tune they seem to be with the land, we don't think it will take too long. In the area where we are landing, it's currently about halfway through their sixteen hours of daylight."

"Love getting ready to greet some territorial aliens without knowing any bloody verbs or adjectives or the way to say 'friendly humans, please don't eat us,'" I muttered darkly, and Theresa gave me a comforting pat on the knee. At least, she was trying to be comforting. But I could see that my words had worried her. I wasn't the only one who thought my lack of acquired alien language skill could potentially fuck us over big time.

The colonel gave a few more instructions, reminding us of things we already knew – no aggressive, sudden movements, only get as close as necessary to communicate – before he took his seat in one of the main console chairs facing the windshield.

"Here we go. Commence descending protocols."

Descending to the planet's surface was indeed nothing like the movies. It was about as rocky as an airplane coming down. We got a little jostled, but before we knew it we had landed, clouds of coppery dust rising from the sand was we did so.

The colonel stood, grinning, then shrugged into his own solar protection jacket, turning to face us with triumphantly open arms.

"Everyone, welcome to -"

An ear-splitting crash and an inhuman shriek split the air. Glass exploded in towards us, and something sharp and bloody and black burst through the front of Colonel Jackson's chest, tearing his uniform and leaving him slumped to the ground when whatever it was withdrew.

Screams rang out around us, as did more of the catastrophic shrieking, like metal grating against metal.

I could barely process what was going on. Colonel Jackson, along with all the pilots and soldiers who had been at the front of the bridge, were on the ground, dead and bleeding. My mouth dropped open in horror as I finally clued into why.

Alien creatures that I couldn't identify were pouring into the shattered windshield opening. There were like nothing I'd ever seen on earth – a metre tall, at least, resembling some kind of coconut crab/spider/scorpion mashup. Their powerful, armoured black legs scrabbled into the room, stabbing soldiers with their spiked tails as they did so.

I was frozen to the spot, as was Theresa, but Melanie sprang up. Kat quickly followed, and they yanked at our elbows.

"Get *the fuck* up," Kat screamed over the sounds, and I shook myself, jumping onto shaky legs.

"We gotta go," Melanie said. Her voice was strangely smooth and unperturbed.

The other girls were all also jumping to their feet now. The remaining soldiers were firing their guns towards the horrific creatures, but that seemed to do nothing at all. *I mean, they were strong enough to crash through a goddamn spaceship's wall. Don't see what a bullet will do.*

Kat seemed to have the same thought.

"We're on another planet, on a spaceship out of the goddamn future, and all you guys have are shitty guns?" She screamed her question at Chapman, who was closest to us, standing between us and the creatures, firing her pistol over and over. Her face was pale, her jaw set, as she pulled the trigger again and again and again.

"Dude, *open the fucking door*," Kat yelled at Chapman, pounding against the doors we'd entered through just a short while ago. Everyone was now crowding around the doors, scratching and yanking at the smooth surface. A muscle in Chapman's jaw jumped, but she kept firing. The crab creatures had gotten distracted with their first kills, stopping to start eating the people who'd fallen at the front of the bridge, but they made short work of those bodies, advancing towards us once again.

"We're gonna be next," I shouted, grabbing Chapman's shoulder and shaking as hard as I could. This seemed to startle her out of her gun-happy reverie. Her gaze swung between her fallen comrades and us.

"Fuck it. I did not sign up for this," she muttered, yanking the key badge from her pocket once again and smashing it against the screen at the doors. They slid open, and we all fell through the doors in a tangled mass of panicked limbs. Chapman ushered everyone forward, screaming at us to, "go, go, go!" while she kept her gun trained on the creatures that were almost upon us. Just as one was reaching its barbed tail towards her, she vaulted through the doors while at the same time flipping the key badge against the screen. The doors slid shut, trapping one of the creature's scrabbling black legs. I had assumed the leg would snap at the force of the doors closing, but rather, it was using its ferocious alien strength to pry those doors back open.

"That won't hold for long. Let's go!" Shouted Chapman, brandishing her gun forwards. "Follow me!"

No one had time for questions. We all fell in behind her, sprinting down the hallway. She was the only soldier left. Since she'd been standing at the back with all of us, she'd been somewhat safe. Everyone else on the bridge was gone. *Holy fuck. It's literally just us now.*

Chapman led us to the other side of the ship, entering what appeared to be some kind of cargo bay: a large, open room with supplies and boxes lining the walls. She ran over to a keypad at one end of the room and started frantically typing before smashing her key badge against its small screen. A massive metallic click rang out, followed by a loud rolling sound, like a garage door being opened. I gasped to see the far wall of the cargo bay sliding up into the body of the ship. Sunlight poured in.

"Wait, that's the plan?" I shouted as she ran towards the exit. "We're going out there?"

Chapman whirled back. We all crowded in towards each other, a crying, shaking group, while Chapman stared.

"You want to stay in here? Be my guest. But those things were powerful enough to smash through our reinforced screens. Screens that can withstand space travel. There's nowhere in this place you can hide where they won't find you. I'm not hiding in here and waiting to die. I'm gonna run."

She used her gun to point to the now open side of the cargo bay.

"Come with me or don't. It's up to you."

With that, she started sprinting. With a curse, Kat followed her, then Melanie, as did some of the other girls.

My stomach churned, and with a sickening ache in my chest, I realized I'd left my pack behind. No food. No water. No nothing.

But Chapman had a gun and maybe some sort of plan. That was something.

"She's right," I said to the others, about half the group that were still standing with me in the cargo bay. "Those crab things are going to tear this ship apart looking for us. We have to run." I didn't want to leave anyone behind if I could help it, but I had no doubt the sound of the doors opening was going to attract those things to this side of the ship at any second. We had to go. Now.

Theresa sobbed, but grabbed my hand and nodded, her tears tracking watery blue lines through her sunscreen.

"Hope you paid attention in your Alien 101 classes," she choked out as we started to run, followed by the others. My jaw tightened grimly as we made it out onto the brutally hot sand. Oh, I'd paid attention all right. I'd done my level fucking best.

I just hoped to God that it would be enough.

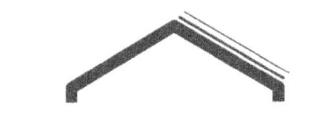

CHAPTER FOUR
Buroudei

It had been more than fourteen days since the Lavrika had called me to the pools. Fourteen times the sun had chased the broken line of moons from one side of the sky to the other. Fourteen days of coming back to the Cliffs of Uruzai searching for clues. Searching for something. Anything. Anything that might give me more information about the strange vision of my even stranger mate.

It was getting harder and harder to think of excuses to come here alone. Even Galok, who trusted me implicitly, was growing concerned. Every time I told him I was leaving to patrol our borders, or to hunt, he'd look at me strangely. "Let the hunters and guards do that, Buroudei. The Gahn should not concern himself with such mundane tasks," he'd said, looking at me as if I'd gone half-mad. And maybe I had gone mad. I'd never before been so consumed with such a singular need. The need for answers. The need to see that small, pale face again.

I adjusted my positioning atop my mount, my irkdu, its massive long body moving easily over the sand, as we approached the Cliffs of Uruzai yet again. As we got close to the cliff's opening, the Lavrikala stationed there eyed me warily, but said nothing. The Lavrikala had grown used to my daily visits. I never dismounted, never tried to enter the caves, and so the sacred guards largely let me be as I stalked back and forth on my animal. It was pointless to try to enter the caves again now. Warriors were only permitted inside at the invitation of the Lavrika. Otherwise, only our female healers were allowed to enter at will, to replenish their supplies of Lavrika's blood.

Perhaps the Lavrika has lied to me. Shown me some falsehood I should ignore.

But no, such thoughts were blasphemy. Generations ago, our ancestors had ignored the visions of the Lavrika. And it had almost destroyed us, decimating our numbers. We were nowhere near recovered from those mistakes.

I sighed, staring first at the sand, then the sky.

Nothing. Nothing new. Everything just the same as before.

Wait.

I squinted, my gaze narrowing in on a strange dark shape in the distance. It was descending from the sky, and as it got closer to the ground, I heard a deep, unfamiliar whirring sound.

My mount bucked and wriggled, its animal senses picking up on the thing in the sky. Wordlessly, I pulled my axe from its loop on my belt, and gripped my spear, leaning forward. The Lavrikala widened her stance, readying her spear, her eyes cast upward, looking worried but determined.

"I will go," I called to her. Whatever this was, whatever threat, I would put myself between it and the Lavrikala and the caves.

The creature flew, as if it were a krixel, but it had no wings to speak of. And at this distance, the fact it looked as large as it did, meant it was bigger than any krixel, bigger than any creature I had ever seen. It had a round, flat body that reminded me of the discs our cubs threw back and forth for sport. When it landed, the whole ground shook, and my irkdu groaned and tossed its head. I tightened my thighs against its body, keeping it under control, then clicked my tongues, axe and spear at the ready.

My irkdu shot forward, its many legs working swiftly over the surface of the sand. There was no time to return to the tents and to gather my men about me; we were almost at the fallen flying thing. But when I heard the vicious screams of the zeelk, and saw them burrowing up out of the sand and scuttling towards the fallen creature, I stopped short, whistling for my irkdu to heel, wishing that I had my men around me after all. The zeelk were monstrous, brutal things that could tear even the strongest Sea Sand warrior to pieces. With my irkdu at my side, I could handle a few of the things on my own. But there were more than ten scrabbling towards the strange fallen creature. I had no reason to throw myself into that fray, and I held back, watching with keenly guarded eyes, my hands still tight on my weapons.

There was a see-through shelf of bone at the front of the fallen thing, and the zeelk crashed through it, moving into the body of the huge beast. The creature did not seem to be alive after its landing, and I saw no blood running from its wounds. The zeelk were all inside the thing now, and I could hear their terrible shrieks alongside terrific crashes. And then more screams – lighter and softer, working deep into my bones. My chest clenched, my grip tightening so hard against my weapons that my knuckles cracked. There were other things inside the great beast. Creatures that were still alive.

Suddenly, the other side of the fallen beast split along an invisible seam, and its shining skin pulled back and up. My irkdu snuffled and growled, but I held it steady, eyes narrowing. I expected zeelk to spill out of that new opening, as if the fallen creature was expelling them somehow. But what I saw instead brought everything around me to a powerful, grinding halt.

A two-legged creature in strange clothing sprinted from the newly opened belly. The hood of her clothing fell back revealing a pale face, and a guttural snarl ripped from my throat. *Could it be...?*

But no, this creature had hair the colour of flames. My mate had looked different. But there was no denying this fire-haired creature was of the same people as my mate. She stumbled in the sand, pausing and looking back, and more creatures like her followed, all appearing to be female, their hides ranging from the palest pink to deep brown, the hair on their heads coming in all different shades and shapes and textures. One of them seemed to have no hair on her head at all. I scanned the group, but none of them seemed to be the one I'd seen in the Lavrika Pools. Fear, something I had not felt since I was a cub, clawed at my guts. Fear at the thought that my mate could be trapped somewhere in the beast, or murdered by foul zeelk. I gave a cry, and my irkdu charged forward.

Another group of women was running from the fallen beast, now. And at the front of their running line, I saw her. And it was like everything else ceased to exist. There was no sea of sand, no zeelk, no sky or sun or cliffs. There was only her, shining like a single star in darkness. Shining like a beacon, a sign, a glorious explosion of destiny. *My mate.* Every part of my body pounded with this new reality, sacred strength surging through me, culminating in a vicious scream that tore from my chest as my irkdu plunged forward.

My mate was holding onto another female, and that other female stumbled and fell. My mate whipped around, her long light-coloured hair flying around her head in a strange and beautiful cloud, and she called something I could not understand, reaching back for her peer. But then the zeelk were following, screaming and skittering out of the slashed belly the women had just come from. One zeelk was heading right for the two of them, and a fearsome rage unlike anything I'd ever known burst inside me, flooding every limb with dark heat. I hefted my spear, its point made from the barb of a zeelk I'd killed in my youth, the only thing that could damage their black armour. Our ablik weapons were strong and sharp, but they could only inflict damage when aimed perfectly at the zeelk's exposed joints.

I cocked my arm and my spear shot forward, crashing into the zeelk with deadly accuracy. The miserable creature collapsed, its legs crunching in on its body in the death grip of my weapon. I yanked an ablik knife from the dakrival hide straps criss-crossing over my back, and hurled it at another nearby zeelk. But it clanged off the armour. I gritted my fangs, pulling another knife and throwing it, trying to keep my aim steady as my irkdu charged forward.

This knife found its target, slipping between the zeelk's body armour and the spot where its leg emerged. It screamed and collapsed, trying to move through the sand with its wounded leg. It wasn't dead, but close enough for now.

My eyes swung back to my mate. She was pulling the fallen woman. The one who had fallen seemed to be in hysterics. I growled in anger. She was slowing my mate down and hindering her escape. But even then I felt a small swell of pride. My mate was no coward.

I had almost reached the group now, but I had no other plan. There was no way for me to take on all these zeelk alone. I only had a few more blades at my back. My priority now was to get my mate out of the fray and away from here as quickly as possible. But that would mean leaving her kind behind, and that was something that could not stand.

Get her first. The rest comes later.

The fire-haired woman had circled back, helping lift the fallen woman. In her hand she held a black object. It looked like it could have been carved from ablik, with a long, snout-like opening. As another zeelk scuttled towards them I readied myself to throw my axe, but before I could do so she aimed the snouted thing at the zeelk, and a series of terrific bangs clanged through the air. The weapon, or whatever it was, was still in her hand, and yet it seemed like she had somehow gotten a successful shot into one of the breaks in the zeelk's armour. It faltered, then fell, mere steps from the small group. The other women were running in every direction as more zeelk charged from the fallen beast's belly.

I was almost upon them, now, almost able to reach my tiny mate, down on the sand, when the fire-haired woman turned and saw me. Her strange-coloured eyes grew wide, and she said something to the others, raising her ablik snout weapon and aiming it directly at my chest. I ignored her. No weapon would make me falter now. Not even a hundred thousand zeelk would keep me from the woman with the long, light hair. I heard the ablik snout thing make a small click sound, and the fire-haired woman gave an agonized scream, throwing it to the sand.

And then they were running. All three of them, along with the others, spreading out and sprinting over the sand, away from the wreckage, away from the zeelk. And from me.

Why does she run from me?

My mate's tiny, narrow feet sunk into the sand with every step. She would never be able to outrun the zeelk, let alone my irkdu, whose many legs were perfectly primed to skim over the sand with ease. Yet still, she tried, her legs pumping, hair flying behind her. The tenacity was equally appealing as it was irritating. I liked witnessing the fire of spirit that made her run against all odds. But I did not appreciate that she was currently running from me.

My irkdu was at her side, and with a swing of my upper body, I leaned down, scooping her up with one arm, holding my axe at the ready with the other.

"You are safe now," I said, tossing her across my lap, her small, tight rump high in the air. She was smaller than I'd originally thought, much smaller than I'd been able to tell she was in the vision of the pools. She screamed something, kicking fiercely, rotating so that she was lying lengthwise along the irkdu, her feet colliding ineffectually with my chest as she seemed to simultaneously attempt to buck off of the mount and hold on for dear life.

With my free hand, I gripped the back of her strange clothing and yanked her upright so that she was in a sitting position between my thighs. And still she fought, her short, blunted claws digging into the forearm I'd locked around her torso. Such a show of spirit would normally have been amusing. But here, now, where the zeelk were all around us in the sand, it was… complicating things. Not that it was difficult to subdue her. No, not at all. Despite her fierce energy, she was much smaller than me, and much, much weaker. It was no trouble for me to keep her safely seated with my one arm, her slim back firm against my chest. But it was distracting me. Her flailing kept causing me to lose focus, her hair flying into my eyes, obscuring my view. And I needed to see. I had good hearing, but her screaming and the chaotic sounds of the sands was dulling any extra help my ears would have lent me.

Her head shot back, catching my throat making me cough, just as a long strip of her hair flitted across my eyes, causing me to blink.

"Get your hair under control, woman, or I will be forced to sheer it off with my blade."

The thought of changing anything about her physically pained me, but as stray strands of her hair got sucked into my mouth, causing me to choke, I realized that it may be necessary.

She screamed something else, and a moment later a slight pain, like the prick of a drizelfly's stinger, pinged in my forearm.

She was biting me.

I grinned. I'd seen those tiny blunt teeth in the Lavrika pool. They would do no damage to my tough hide. She bit down harder, and I ignored her.

At least with her head down like that her hair is out of my eyes.

Her mouth occupied meant she'd stopped screaming, too, and was now emitting a low sort of grunt as she tried to break through my skin. Now that her voice wasn't all around me, I could hear more of what was going on, and I sucked in a triumphant breath when I heard a warrior's call, and the sound of many irkdu roaring as they charged. With a click of my tongues and a shift in my thighs, I steered my irkdu to turn, ready to greet my men.

Only it wasn't my men. I squinted, still holding tight to my squirming, biting woman, as about fifteen warriors on irkdu charged forward on the horizon, axes raised and spears flying.

Gahn Fallo's men. A hunting party, by the looks of things.

They were felling zeelk left and right, and scooping up women as they moved through the carnage. I watched the scene unfold, bringing my irkdu to a stop, wondering if I should approach them. But they were just as likely to try to tear me apart as the zeelk would be. Normally I'd relish a chance to clash weapons with Gahn Fallo's men, but fifteen-to-one was bad odds, even for me. Besides, I had my mate to think of, now, and her safety was the only priority. I watched as the last running woman was yanked onto an irkdu and the remaining zeelk fell. It wasn't ideal that they were grabbing hold of all the new female creatures, but it was better than those frail small females getting devoured by zeelk. I had my mate, safe in my arms, and had no reason to linger. With a cry, I urged my irkdu back on track, and we departed over the sands.

As we got further from the fray, and I could relax some of my warrior instincts, I was finally able to fully take in the sensation of having my mate pressed against me. Even the useless bite of her tiny teeth felt good, and I tightened my arm's hold on her, revelling in the feeling of her pert ass scooting harder against my groin. There was nothing better than taking a woman after battle, when your body was still on fire with the brutal action, and my cock was already ready, stretching the dakrival hide loincloth to its limits. But my mate did not seem as keen. She had released my arm, leaving an adorably small set of indentations from her teeth, and she was once again screaming something I could not understand, the words falling and flowing, quick and slippery, like blood through my fingers. Though I could not see her face, as she faced forward and away from me, she seemed, by the sound of her soft, high voice, to be angry.

"Why are you upset? Can you not see that I have saved you from the zeelk?"

Another rush of angry-sounding words crashed from her mouth, and I could only assume that she either did not see that, or did see it, and somehow was still not pleased.

It is possible that my mate is more... difficult... than I had hoped.

Either that, or she was foolish beyond measure. Surely she did not want to be left back with the zeelk?

I needed to try to speak to her. To look into her strange eyes. To impress upon her the ferocity of our new connection. The importance of it. To impress upon her that fighting me was futile.

Not here.

Being out on the open sands like this was not a good idea, not when I could see how painfully fragile she was. We headed back towards the Cliffs of Uruzai. The front area held the entry to the Lavrika Pools, but the cliffs were a truly massive rock formation, and around the other side there were caverns and valleys and small patches of valok plants. The krixel nested there, but if we stayed on the ground and did not climb, it would be safe enough. We forged forward and after some time, time marked by continued fighting, biting, and scratching, we reached the other side of the cliffs. I nudged my irkdu forward, entering the narrow valley between this part of the cliffs, the walls jutting up on either side with unfathomable power. Eventually, I steered us into a narrow crack I knew well, a crack that led to a small, hidden, sunlit area with valok plants growing around the edges. In that small, round space, I directed my irkdu to stop and I dismounted, taking my female with me as I did so. I held her tightly – now that she was on the ground she had renewed her fight, practically jumping out of my grasp, her feet flying from the ground as she bucked and wriggled. I could not suppress the thought – *will she have this much energy when sharing a bed with me?*

I still held my axe in my other hand, the hand not busy keeping my mate under control. With the flat of the blade, I patted my irkdu's back, letting it know it could go graze for peet grass, the tough stuff that sustained it. It curled tightly in the cramped space then moved back through the crack we'd come through. I knew it would not go far from its master.

The creature bucking wildly against, me, though, was another story entirely. I had no doubt that she would do anything in her power to get as far from me as possible as soon as given the chance. What I couldn't understand was why. When a warrior visited the Lavrika Pools and saw a vision of his mate, it awakened the bond within his mate, too. At least, that was how it worked for the people of the Sea Sands. But my mate was not of the Sea Sands.

I positioned us so that I was between the crack, the only exit, and her, and finally let go. As predicted, she ran from me, turning and plastering herself against the cliff wall across from me, her back to the rock. Though every drop of blood in my body longed to go to her and touch her again, I let my hands fall to my sides, hooking my axe back into my belt.

Finally, I got to take in her face. Her real face, solid and pale and perfect before me, lit up by the shining Zaphrinax sun. Her eyes were even more brilliant than they'd been in the pools, and her laughably slim, flat brows were turned down in fierce anger, her small pink mouth open and panting. Her eyes flitted from me to the crack, then around the space, looking for an escape. My strangely pretty mate had not yet learned that there would be no escape from me.

A growl built in the back of my throat, but I forced it down, adjusting the tight fabric at my groin. Though everything in me raged to take her, take her *now*, I would not. Not when displeasure was so plain across her face.

Her face...

My heart clenched as I noticed how much paler she looked than she had in the pools. There was an odd blue substance coating her skin. Blood? Her skin was pale, so maybe her blood was strangely pale, too. I crossed the space between us in one easy step, caging her against the wall with my body, bringing my hands to the sides of her tiny jaw, examining her scalp, her face, for injuries. I found none, and some of the blue-white stuff rubbed off on my hands. Some kind of war paint perhaps. I snorted. Though she'd fought me with admirable spirit, she did not seem to be much of a warrior. Not a properly trained one, at least.

She had frozen totally still, her breath coming in short, quick puffs through her funny raised nose. I kept looking, moving aside her hair, my eyes sweeping over her skin for injuries when I saw it. What looked to be a small gash, just below her tiny, low ear. I hissed as a small red pearl of liquid slipped out, joining the scarlet trail that ran down her impossibly thin neck. A neck that could be crushed in an instant. For a moment, I felt sick at my mate's fragility.

I moved my fingers up, gently probing the wound, being careful of my claws. Her skin was incredibly soft, delicate as the petals of a rindla plant. One wrong move would shred her. My lip twitched, and she gasped as I brushed the wound, her blood seeping against the pads of my fingers. I'd never seen blood this colour – this exquisite scarlet, the same colour as axrekal berries, one of Zaphrinax's most potent poisons. I raised my fingers to my lips, tasting her, the sharp, intoxicating flavour exploding on the three segments of my tongue. The growl returned at the back of my throat, this time less easily quelled, and my cock ached. I held her gaze as I licked my fingers again, her soft pink eyelids widening around the white part of her eyes. Then, though I knew it may make her angry, though I knew it may make her try to flee from me, I groaned and lowered my mouth to her neck, gently lapping the stuff from her soft skin.

What a strange and sublime creature fate had chosen as my mate. A creature with skin the colour of milk. And blood the colour of poison.

Never had I known, in all my war-filled life, a poison quite this sweet. So sweet I'd gladly let it kill me. Over and over again.

CHAPTER FIVE
Cece

Fuck me sideways. Apparently these aliens were vampire aliens. How had no one figured that out yet, with all the data we'd collected? I didn't even know I was bleeding until this guy/alien/thing had collected the blood on his fingers and fucking *licked it*. And now his tongue – a tongue forked into three freaking parts, was working steadily away at my neck. I was completely frozen, scared that one wrong move would change this interaction from one of tongues to one of teeth. His gigantic hands were on me, one holding the side of my face, the other at my hip. There was something undeniably sexual about the positioning of our bodies, and when his very, very hard cock (at least, that's what I assumed it was) pressed against my abdomen, I sucked in a breath. *I'm in trouble.*

I had to get out of this situation. I had to do something. I was about to be fucked. Or food. Maybe not even in that order. *Oh, God.*

His tongue, or one part of it, at least, caught the edge of the cut on my neck and electricity shot through me, arching down my spine. I cast my mind about for a way to get out of this. There was no way I could escape or physically overpower this monster. I gave a small cry as his tongue moved lower, exploring my collarbone beneath my jacket.

Tongue. Tongue! Language!

What words had I learned? My brain seemed to have gone completely blank. *Come on, come on...*

"Ablik!" The word exploded out of me, and the alien froze. "Ahbluhk? Oblique?" I couldn't remember the exact pronunciation now. But it seemed to have worked either way. The alien slowly drew back. My skin was hot where his mouth had been, and instinctively I reached up, my hand smacking against the flesh and staying there. I felt the slow ooze of blood and the dampness of his saliva against my palm as I stared at my captor, taking in his form, in detail, for the first time.

His skin was a deep copper, fading to brown, and even as dark as black at certain points, like his shoulders, his feet, and the end of his tail. Yup. A tail. It was long, but not skinny like a cat's. It was as thick as one of his massive thighs at the base, tapering to a dark, firm point, almost like a kangaroo's, but without fur. His feet, too, were oddly kangaroo-esque – long and dark, with one long central claw and two smaller ones on the sides, his ankle high, strangely bent, and strong. His hands seemed mostly human-like, with four fingers and a thumb on each, but with black claws that looked like they could rend my flesh without even trying. From his shins to his shoulders he looked mostly like a man – a massive man, though, packed with hard muscle and easily seven feet tall. I craned my neck to look at his face. The bottom half – the strong, sharp jaw, and the mouth, were mostly familiar, besides the fangs and tongues, at least. But the top half of his face was where things got... weird.

His nose was largely flat, flaring open and down like a cat's. His brows were heavy, raised, and dark, the skin fading from bronze to black as it met his dark hairline, his hair falling in one thick, black braid down his muscled back. At the top of his head, on the sides, his ears stood tall and pointed, like a doberman whose ears had been cropped. And his eyes. What the actual fuck. Those *eyes*. They were like nothing I'd ever seen before. They were large, with no white to speak of. Huge and black, with a shimmering collection of copper-coloured sparks in the middle that swirled, expanded, and contracted. It looked like tiny metallic galaxies existed in those eyes, the stars moving outward and inward, called by some strange gravity. If I weren't worried about having this guy, or animal, or whatever he was, kill me and bury my bones in the desert, I would have admired the foreign beauty of them.

But as it was, I *was* worried about getting killed and dumped in the desert. So I latched onto the one thing that seemed to have caught his attention and slowed him down.

"Ablik!" I said again, my voice squeaking. His ears twitched, and he cocked his huge head, stepping back and letting me go. Before I could breathe a sigh of relief, he pulled a knife from one of the leather-looking straps tied across his torso.

Oh, shit. Had I offended him? What did ablik even mean, again? Was it stick? Weapon? He hefted the knife – more like a machete, though it looked small in his hand. *Uh oh. Maybe he thinks I'm threatening him. Great work.*

"No, no, sorry. I didn't mean ablik. I meant... Um... God, I can't remember any other words. Maybe you could put the knife away for a second, eh? Nice alien..."

He cocked his head again, his brows contracting, the copper specks and swirls drawing in tightly towards the centre of his eyes. It seemed like he was trying to focus in on something.

He held the knife up between us, and I flinched back, my eyes squeezing shut. But no pain came. Instead, his deep, growling voice boomed in the small space, reverberating throughout my body.

"Ablik."

I opened one eye, then the other, lowering my hands as I realized he was pointing at the shining black blade of his knife.

"Ablik," he said again, then he took out his axe, which seemed to be made from the same black material. "Ablik." He pointed to the axe's black blades.

"Oh," I said, relaxing somewhat. So maybe our interpretation had been right. Ablik was weapon? Or maybe the dark material the weapons were made of.

I tentatively reached forward, brushing the flat of the axe with my fingers. The material the blades were made from was incredibly smooth and hard.

"Ablik?"

He gave a thrumming sort of yip, which I imagined must be some kind of confirmation.

OK, cool. We have one word in common so far. What other words did I know? As long as we were talking, he wasn't licking me or doing any other weird stuff. And that was probably good. I ignored the electric thrill that ran under my skin, everywhere his bizarre tongue had touched me. I would have to analyze that feeling later.

"Um... Um... what about valok?" If I remembered correctly, that seemed to be a small ground-dwelling animal that the aliens picked up and ate raw.

His dark brows raised slightly, the shimmering sparks of his eyes moving outwards. He took a step, turning from me, but still keeping himself firmly planted between me and the crack in the wall. *Damn.* But then again, where the hell did I think I was going to escape to? I'd seen what those massive crab things had done to the pilots and soldiers. At least, so far, all this guy had done was lick me. And I'd noticed, in the chaos, the way he'd even managed to take a couple of those creepy crawly bastards out with nothing but his primitive blades, almost like he was protecting me. That is, assuming he wasn't just trying to beat the spideys to a tasty Earth girl meal. My eyes drifted over his slab-of-muscle body, the massive pecs, broad, rippling shoulders, the tree trunk thighs. The loincloth that was still pulled suspiciously tight. *Yikes.* Well, as long as he kept *that* area under control, we'd be golden. *Guess I'll take my chances with kangaroo gladiator dude. For now.*

He replaced his axe at his belt, then bent, using the knife he still held to saw off what seemed to be a plant along the rock wall near my feet. It was small, greyish-green, and looked a heck of a whole lot like an

Earth cactus of some kind. He handled it carefully, avoiding the nasty-looking black barbs on its smooth, dry surface, standing and holding it up between us.

"Valok," he said. Then he took his knife, splitting the cactus thing with the blade and pulling the plant's skins apart, revealing a sticky translucent goo on the inside. Ah. So that's what we'd seen in the footage. It wasn't an animal, but a plant getting split open and having the insides sucked out. Like an alien juice box.

He held the plant out to me, indicating that I should have some, and I shook my head vigorously.

"No thank you, Mr Alien. I have no clue if my human stomach can handle whatever that is."

Speaking of stomachs, mine immediately fell when I remembered that I had no human supplies at all. No water. No food. No sunscreen or backup clothing.

Maybe I can get back to the ship somehow...

Maybe all those crab spider things were gone now. But what about the other women, my friends? I'd been so focused on fighting this guy off when he'd grabbed me, that I had no idea what had happened to the others. Panic rushed through me at the thought.

"We have to go back!" I said quickly, pointing wildly at the crack we'd come through. "Back!"

The kangaroo gladiator guy was looking at me like I was nuts. And maybe I was, to go back there. I'd be putting myself in massive danger, not to mention him. Even though he seemed like he held his own pretty well before. *At the very least, if things went really badly, maybe I can bury them.* The thought of Theresa, Melanie, Kat, and the others, lifeless and alone in the sun, made my stomach clench with nausea.

I shook my head, gritting my teeth. Whatever had happened to them, I had to go back. To get supplies. And see if there were any other survivors.

"Back, let's go *back*." God damn it. How could I tell this massive wall of body what I wanted? I didn't know a single verb or preposition. Just a random dabbling of nouns that, so far, had proven to be kind of off-base. I wasn't even sure that I wanted him to take me back there – I still wasn't clear on his intentions. The massive pull at his loincloth told me whatever his intentions may have been, they were definitely not entirely honourable. But there was no way I'd survive two seconds out there without him.

Well, Cece, you've got yourself in quite the fucking pickle.

My English, combined with the wild gesturing of my arms, wasn't getting us anywhere. Neither were the phrases in Japanese, French, or Spanish that I tossed his way. The alien had tossed the valok plant down and sheathed his knife at his back once more, and was watching me with an unreadable expression. His hands hung loose at his sides, but his entire body thrummed with energy. I knew that the second I tried to make a move, he'd react. How he'd react, I had no idea.

No other way to find out...

I took a sharp breath, then faked movement to one side before sprinting around the other, aiming for the crack we'd come through. I hadn't made it two steps before a rock-hard arm shot out, snaking around my waist, drawing my back hard against the alien's torso. A ripple of guttural language ran through the air, and I was pissed to realize I didn't recognize a single word. *What the fuck kind of training did I get? How they did they have a hope in hell of me communicating with these guys?*

The alien said a bit more, and I shivered at the feeling of his breath against my ear and neck. And there was that erection, pressing into my back.

"OK, OK, my dude. This is not time for... whatever it is you have in mind." His hands ran down to my hips, and I felt his mouth brush along my neck once more, sending heat bursting below my skin and, absurdly, between my legs. A deep, warning growl emanated from him, the sound a strange, primal call that was answered by something deep within my body. I squeezed my thighs together.

For a moment, nothing else happened. I had to admit that, if he'd wanted to kill or eat or rape me, he would have done it by now. There was literally no way I could have stopped him, yet so far he'd done nothing to harm me. Sure, he'd licked the blood from my skin like a weirdo, but he'd also saved me from certain crab-clawed death, and had tried to feed me from the spiky aloe thing. *He has tools, and language, and some kind of domesticated animal he uses as a mount.* And there was no denying the deep, almost unsettling intelligence I'd glimpsed in his strange eyes. *I wish I could talk to him. Fuck you, Colonel Jackson, for all of this.*

But when his huge, hot hands moved, slipping under my jacket and moving up to my waist, it seemed very clear that talking was not what this guy was interested in at the moment. I spun in his grip, placing my hands flat against his pecs, my fingers splayed against the impossibly tough skin. I remembered when he'd first grabbed me, and I'd bitten down as hard as I could, barely making a dent. *What the hell is he made of?*

It wasn't just tough. It was smooth, and warm, and the way it faded in places from copper to brown to black was strangely appealing. For a moment, I forgot what I was meant to be doing, to be saying. That is, until his hands descended to grip my ass.

I yelped, jerking, then smacking my palms against his wall of a chest.

"Stop that!"

His brows contracted, and he said something in his deep, growly voice. His hands moved back up to my waist. But then, a moment later, they were gripping my butt again. He was staring hard at me, the metallic specks of his eyes completely blown apart, turning his whole gaze into something shimmering and uncentred. There was a mischievous sort of curiosity in the angle of his head, the slight uptick of his mouth. *Oh my God, he thinks my reactions are funny.* Anger bubbled up in my chest, and I gave him my best fuck-you face.

"No." I did my best to inject my voice with a dangerous tone, and it sort of seemed like it worked. The metallic glimmers of his eyes immediately contracted inward, and the beginnings of a grin that had been pulling at his mouth disappeared. He said something to me again, something I could not for the life of me understand. I could tell, though, that he was asking me a question. What that question was, was anyone's guess.

"Sorry," I said softly. "I don't have any answers."

His face darkened, but a moment later, he let me go. And this time, he stepped aside, allowing me access to the only exit. I faltered, wondering if this was some sort of trap, but he just seemed to watch me impassively, tracking my every movement.

Alrighty, then.

I moved forward, following the path back out the way we'd come -- and came face to face with a monster.

I reared back as the thing snarled, and raised my hands to protect my face, just as Mr Kangaroo Gladiator made a clicking sound at the back of his throat. The monster snuffed, then turned and moved away, and I watched it warily, my heart in my throat.

It was the thing we'd rode in on, of course. But I hadn't realized how truly creepy the thing was when I'd been on its back.

Its hide was a deep, dusty purple, and its head and body vaguely resembled an Earth alligator, if alligators from Earth had, like, twenty eyes. And instead of four legs, it had what looked to be hundreds, sweeping over the sand like a centipede. It was huge, bigger than any alligator on earth, more like the size of a small whale. With really, really big teeth.

They don't have alien horses where this guy comes from? We have to deal with the dino-centipede?

Despite the heat, I shivered, watching its many insect-like legs move in a horrible ripple. At least it seemed to listen to the alien guy's commands.

I turned back to see said alien guy right behind me, his dark eyes fixed on me. I swallowed, the intensity of that gaze penetrating me.

"I guess I should stop calling you alien guy, eh? What's your name?"

Idiot. Like he'll understand that question.

It was time to pantomime, just like some stupid Tarzan role play. Only instead of role play, this was my real life.

I placed my hand to my chest.

"I'm Celia. Cece. Cece."

I pounded my chest each time to emphasize my point. I was worried I'd have to do this dance a few times, but he seemed to catch my drift pretty quickly. *OK, he's definitely a pretty sharp guy. Or, er, alien.*

He imitated my gesture, placing his own clawed hand against his chest.

"Gahn Buroudei." He, paused, then said a bunch more, the syllables going in one ear and out the other.

"Sorry, I didn't get all that. Got a nickname? I'm Celia, but people call me Cece." I gestured to myself again as I said, "Cece."

He paused, the bright parts of his eyes pulsing, then placed his hand on his chest again.

"Buroudei."

Then he did something strange. His tail curled around the front of his body, the black tip reaching up to cover his eyes for a moment. It was just for a second, and then his tail swished back into place. Not sure what to make of that, I focused on what he'd said.

"Buroudei… OK, yeah, I can handle that. I hope that's actually your name, and you didn't just try to tell me your word for chest or heart or something. Do you even have a heart? Nevermind."

My sentence fizzled. Still he watched me, something dark and deep and unnameable in his alien eyes.

Then he opened his mouth, his voice somewhere between a growl and a purr, and said,

"Zeezee."

My name in his mouth was terrible and gratifying. Bizarre and enticing. It sent heat down my spine and goosebumps over my skin. It felt like he was recognizing something deep inside me. As if he knew something about me that even I didn't.

And, frankly, I didn't like it one fucking bit.

CHAPTER SIX
Buroudei

Not for the first time, I began to wonder if the Lavrika was playing some cruel trick. It had ignited the sacred mate bond inside me, but, it appeared, not inside my mate, my Zeezee. Such a thing was unheard of among my people. People had rejected their mates before, and rejected their bonds, but it was at least there to be rejected. My strange little mate didn't seem to feel anything at all. At least, she didn't seem to feel anything besides fear and anger and the need to run. This was puzzling. *She* was puzzling. And not only was this confusing and complicated, but it was also heart-rending. The men who'd told me of this bond's power, who'd warned me of this lovesickness, had not exaggerated. My entire body, my very existence, was for her, now. How could she not see that? And how could she not feel the same?

And so, when she'd spoken to me so firmly, so angrily, I'd let her go. For the moment, anyway. I did not intend to let her go far. I would observe her, learn her ways, and teach her what it meant to be the mate of a mighty Gahn. Soon she would see. She had to.

I did not like to think of what would happen if she didn't.

She was talking to me, her words coming quick and lovely from her soft mouth. It amazed me that she could speak so swiftly with only one tongue segment. The wide, pink thing was more agile than I would have guessed. I followed her as she continued to walk, back out from the cliffs and onto the sand. She scanned the horizon with her gleaming eyes, then pointed, turning back to me.

I followed her arm, my eyes settling on the wreckage of the fallen beast in the distance.

Ah. So she wanted to return to that thing. To the scene of the almost-slaughter. I growled, and her brows contracted in what appeared to be irritation.

"I will not take you back there. It is not safe, my Zeezee."

More mysterious sounds trilled from her pretty mouth, but I was resolute. None of her charms would sway me on this matter. Although, she did not seem intent on using any of her charms. She spat some of her words at me, harshly, then turned and started walking. I waited for a moment, to see what she would do, but she did not turn back, simply continuing in a straight line onto the sand. A muscle jumped in my jaw. *She will not stop. She will not turn back.*

I ignored the painful lurch in my chest at the thought that she could walk away, leaving me without looking back. I couldn't think about what that meant now. What I did have to think about was her safety. Safety that was being risked with every step she took.

With a few sprinting steps, I caught up with her, grabbing onto her hand. She stopped short, whirling on me. I tried to imitate a gesture she'd done earlier, when she'd been expressing her displeasure at my actions. Her head had swung back and forth, quickly. I did the same, the feeling a strange one. She paused, her expression softening as I did so, and a thrill ran through me. The thrill turned to concern, though, when I noticed that the places on her face that I had wiped the war paint from had become very red.

That... cannot be good.

I cast my eyes over her clothing, noting the hood at the back of her strange cloak. Maybe it was some sort of facial protection. Though what could be hurting her face, I did not know. And not knowing filled me with brooding worry. I grabbed the funny, stiff fabric in my hands, pulling the hood up over her head, settling it firmly and carefully. She watched me closely as I did so, worrying at her pink bottom lip with her unimpressive teeth.

Strange. I peered closer. Her skin looked even more red now, and her eyes were wide.

She gave a choked, spluttering kind of sound and turned rapidly, marching away. My mouth flattened as I realized grimly she was going to continue on into danger unless I stopped her. Resigned, I strode forward, picking her up and slinging her easily over my shoulder.

Suffice to say, she was not pleased.

More kicking and screaming ensued, with angry words I could make out but not understand. *Ahh-sole. Tie-rent.*

I gave a low whistle, calling my irkdu to us, and mounted the thing easily, even with Zeezee on my shoulder.

"You can ride upright, as you did before, or stay tossed over my shoulder like a misbehaving cub. The choice is yours."

She paused, listening, then strung together a long, fiery sentence before her kicking finally ceased. Satisfied, I slid her down and around, so that she was nestled between my thighs once more. My cock pulsed insistently, but I ignored it, cursing whatever black luck had left me with me with a mate whom I could not understand and who did not seem to want me. But as I tucked my arm protectively around her slim waist, pulling her to me and feeling the rise and fall of her breath against my chest, I didn't really feel unlucky. Fate had bestowed something sacred and strange upon me. It was up to me to make it all make sense. My cock throbbed once more and I sighed, urging my irkdu forward.

This was going to be a very long ride.

《 》

WE HAD A LOT OF GROUND to cover before we reached the tents of my people. Some of the journey was made in the shadow of the cliffs, but much of it had to take place over the open sands. I kept my axe at the ready, keenly aware of my surroundings. I lamented the loss of my spear. It had been a brutal weapon. But, I consoled myself, once I had gathered some of my men, we could take a safer trip back to the scene of the zeelk killings and get many more spear tips. Assuming Gahn Fallo's men hadn't stripped everything bare after taking the women.

The women. That was an issue I would have to return to. In the midst of the battle, I'd been happy to let Gahn Fallo's men take them as long as it meant no more foul zeelk were nipping at my mate's slender heels. But I was growing more and more convinced that the reason Zeezee wanted to go back the way we'd come was to find her fellow tribeswomen. I remembered the way she'd tried to help the other fallen woman, trying to pull her up and to safety. Yes, she would not be happy until we had recovered the other women. But that would take time to prepare for, and a coordinated effort. I would do it for her. Of course I would. But we needed men. And a plan.

And, if I were being honest with myself, I wouldn't just be doing it to please Zeezee. If one of these females could be chosen as my mate, then perhaps others could be mated to the men of my tribe. In our tribe there was only one woman for every three males of mating age. This could be the greatest blessing our tribe had seen in generations. My optimism soured, however, when I realized Gahn Fallo would likely be thinking the same thing for his own men. He was a vicious enemy, but he was no fool.

Zeezee had been talking almost without end for the entire ride, but my ears pricked as I realized she had fallen silent. I'd been so focused on watching the sands for any sign of movement that I hadn't noticed when she'd stopped. The sun was setting, the broken line of moons rising, casting everything into smoky shadows. The stars blinked in a bruised sky. Zeezee was leaning against me, now, her full weight relaxed against my chest and abdomen. The sensation made my heart surge. Was she finally feeling what I felt? Was she experiencing the sacred bond? She was closer to me, willingly, than she'd ever been. *This must mean something.*

I was bending my head, muttering her name against her hood, my arm tightening around her waist when I smelled it. The scent normally intoxicating, but in this moment, horrific.

Zeezee's blood.

CHAPTER SEVEN
Cece

The sun was setting, I had no idea where the fuck we were or where the fuck we were going, and I *did not* feel good. Thankfully Buroudei had pulled my forgotten hood up to help shield me from this planet's wicked sun (and did so in such a bizarre, almost tender, way that I'd almost toppled over) but I still felt completely unprepared for this environment. I was beyond hot under my solar protection jacket, but I knew I couldn't take it off with that sun beating down and no extra sunscreen. My throat was growing more dry by the second, and I was starting to regret having refused the cactus juice box I'd been offered hours before.

It has been hours, right? My sense of time was completely shot. It felt like we'd been moving over the same stretch of sand for days. My thighs were on fire, my skin rubbing painfully beneath my pants against the animal we were riding, and my muscles were cramping so hard my legs were starting to go numb. Buroudei seemed to straddle this giant thing with ease. He didn't even have pants or chaps or a saddle or anything. But he was much larger than me, with longer legs, and skin like some kind of reinforced alien leather. For my weak, stumpy human legs, the positioning was awkward and painful as all get out.

Not like there was much else I could do, though, so I sucked it up. As best I could, anyway. But by the time the stars were starting to peek out overhead, I'd reached my limit. I sagged back against Buroudei, for once not fighting him, grateful for the solid stability his rock-hard body provided, my head swimming, my chapped lips parting as I panted. The sky, the sand, everything was growing black in my dimming vision.

I'm just going to close my eyes...

"Zeezee!"

Buroudei's voice was a brutal snarl, his hands insistent as he dismounted and pulled me with him. He tried to stand me up on the sand, but at that moment every bone in my body turned to jello and I collapsed, crying out in pain. Head pounding, mouth full of cotton, I looked down and groaned.

The pant legs of my grey uniform were caked with blood, stuck to my inner thighs. The fabric was still intact, but my skin beneath it clearly wasn't, rubbed raw by hours on the back of dino-centipede. I was in a lot worse shape than I had thought, and I flopped back against the sand, defeated. *What is the freaking point of all this?* It would have been so easy to just lay there and never get up again.

Well, it would have been easy if a certain alien weren't going into nuclear meltdown mode above me. He was kneeling at my side, his face twisted in a manic snarl, growling and snapping his jaws, the glimmery bits of his eyes pulled so tight they almost looked like normal irises. Almost.

"You have pretty eyes," I mumbled. It felt like I was floating. Or sinking. Maybe this was all a messed up dream. *Maybe I got hit by a car on my run and I'm in some crazy limbo. Maybe this is Hell.*

But as Buroudei picked me up once again, his arms like iron yet somehow gentle, it didn't really feel like I was in Hell. *If this is Hell, at least I'm not alone.*

I was vaguely aware of Buroudei leaping back onto his mount. Instead of sitting me up the way I had been, he kept me cradled tightly against his chest, and for an absurd moment I felt almost safe, almost whole, something I hadn't felt since Grammy had died.

Buroudei urged his animal to go faster, it seemed, with short, commanding barks, but his voice when he spoke to me, his lips moving against the fabric of my hood, was quiet, though strained. He held me in his massive, metal-strong arms as if I were something precious and breakable. I let my head flop against his warm chest, nuzzling in for the warmth. Now that it was growing dark, I was no longer sweating, and was shivering violently. This seemed to bother him, and he tightened his grip on me, as if he could stop me shivering through sheer force of muscled will. I almost laughed. If anyone could do such a thing, it probably would have been this guy.

I turned my face in towards his chest, my nose and lips, then forehead, brushing the smooth but oh-so tough skin. I felt his muscles tense under my mouth as I whispered, "So, so warm."

And it was then, and only then, that I finally closed my eyes and let the blackness swallow me whole. But that blackness wasn't cold. Not at all. It cradled me with warm arms and echoed with the alien whisper of my name.

CHAPTER EIGHT
Buroudei

Curse me. Curse me ten thousand aching times. Curse my idiocy and my ignorance and my pride. For thinking I could claim this strange creature so easily with no harm done. My stupidity knew no bounds, and now my mate was torn open and bleeding. *How can she possibly be so soft and breakable?* It defied everything that made sense, everything I knew. If this was some kind of test the Lavrika had set before me, I was most certainly failing. And I was failing my mate, which was the most unacceptable part of it all.

I hissed, then growled at my irkdu to go faster, faster, as fast as it could. Its many legs flew, sand spraying behind us as we whipped over the rapidly cooling desert. Zeezee had been shaking in the most alarming way, but now she had gone totally limp, and somehow that was even worse. I bit back a howl of anguish, forging every ounce of worry and sorrow into a dark blade of determination. *I will get her back to the healer in time. There is no other way.*

She could not die. She couldn't. It was impossible. Unthinkable. I would not allow such a thing to happen. She'd only just crashed into my world, but I already knew that there was no way I'd let her leave it now. Not as long as there was breath and blood beating in my body. I'd slain more men than any other in my tribe, had felled zeelk as a cub with nothing but my blades. I was a Gahn among my people. And yet

I knew, I *knew*, with a finality so terrible it made me want to fall to my knees, that I'd be nothing without her.

Thus, I cursed myself. And though it was blasphemous, I cursed the Lavrika, too. For making me so beautifully, painfully vulnerable.

If she dies, there will be no salvation from my rage.

Finally, we approached the tents of my people, when the sky and sand were both drenched black with night. There were about fifty of us in the tribe now: thirty men, ten women, and ten cubs, and the collection of dakrival hide tents was illuminated by the evening fire. Our tribe was currently settled against an outcropping of large boulders, with valok plants and peet grass growing between them. Our irkdu were well trained, and were not restrained when not in use. They moved slowly through the boulders, munching on grass, their duties done for the day.

Most of the tribe would be around the evening fire, now, in the centre of our tiny village of tents. I could only pray that our most experienced healer, an elder woman named Rika, would be there and I wouldn't have to tear the tents apart looking for her.

As I cried for my irkdu to move forward towards our destination, a tall warrior caught my eye, raising his spear in greeting. Galok, my closest friend, was jogging over the sand towards me.

"Buroudei! I was about to cross the sands in search of you. Come, feast with us. The hunters have killed three dakrival today and the best meat has been saved for you."

I clutched Zeezee to my chest – Zeezee, whose skin was mightily cold – and launched off of my irkdu while it was mid-motion, crouching as I landed and springing right back up. Galok's grin faded as he saw us, and he crossed the remaining distance to us with quick steps.

"Buroudei, my friend, what is... what is *this?*"

He peered down at the still bundle in my arms, the sight stars of his eyes pulsing with curious confusion. I had had days to get used to the idea of this creature after seeing her in the Lavrika Pools. But I had told no one what I'd seen, so this female was taking Galok completely by surprise. I would have to save my explanations for another time. Zeezee's blood was all I could smell. The air was choked with it.

"There's no time. I need Rika. Now."

Good Galok, the best of men, understood immediately the seriousness of the situation and nodded stoically, saving his questions.

"Go ahead to the healers' tent. I will find Rika. Go, go!"

I started to run. So too, did Galok, toward the large fire where most of our people were enjoying a meal.

The healers' tent was the largest tent, even larger than my own. No one slept there at night, but during the day the healers, of which we had three, (Rika, Balia, and Balia's cub Zofra, who was training) worked there, preparing salves, making bandages, and treating our people's various ailments. When I reached it, I whipped the tent's flap open so hard I almost tore the tough hide before stepping quickly into the tent's darkness.

Along one side of the tent, shelves built from dakrival bones housed various bits of fabric, herbs, and bowls for pounding and grinding. Beneath the shelves, buried in the sand and out of sight, were jars of Lavrika's blood. There were three dakrival hide beds at the back, and I quickly laid Zeezee in the closest one. Her lips didn't look pink the way they had earlier. They looked greyish, although maybe that was due to the lack of light. I glanced around, finding a candle made from dried valok gel, as well as two pieces of fire rock. I quickly banged them against each other, lighting the valok candle with a spark, and held it near Zeezee's face. The firelight flickered, illuminating each delicate feature – her smooth brow, her high nose. My jaw clenched. I longed to touch her, but was worried any move I made could make things worse. I'd never felt this sickening sense of helplessness before.

At that moment, I heard a rustle behind me, and Rika, closely followed by Galok, entered the tent.

Rika was our oldest female, tall and regal and imposing. She could easily have been a Lavrikala – she was strong enough, even at her advanced age, to serve as a sacred guard. But the Lavrika had not called her to such a post. And our tribe was lucky for it – she was enormously skilled as a healer.

She raised her tail in front of her eyes quickly to greet me respectfully, but I growled, slashing my hand through the air, gesturing that she should stop.

"Do not waste time with formalities, Rika. Look to my female."

Her sight stars, grown silver with age, contracted sharply in her large eyes, and she looked down at Zeezee with a sudden intake of breath. She tossed her long white braid over her shoulder and knelt, sniffing the air, and starting to examine Zeezee's head and face with gentle but firm fingers.

"What is this creature, Gahn Buroudei? Where does she hail from?" Rika asked quietly.

Galok had stepped forward, standing beside me, staring down with a disturbed sort of fascination.

"I do not know. She, and others like her, emerged from some sort of fallen flying beast, out past the Cliffs of Uruzai. They were attacked by zeelk, of which I felled two. I took this woman just as Gahn Fallo's men arrived. They killed the other zeelk and took the rest of the females."

I could feel Galok's questioning stare from beside me, but I ignored him. My attention was completely absorbed by my small, still mate.

"She is bleeding. Her legs, Rika, look there first. Get the Lavrika's blood, she needs quick healing."

But Rika shook her head, her hands continuing to explore with maddening slowness.

"She is like no creature of the Sea Sands. I have never seen one like her. I do not know if our healing methods will work. I must examine her further."

Impatient panic exploded in my chest, and I growled, prowling back and forth in the tent as Rika looked at the fabric of Zeezee's strange clothing.

"She is breathing, and she has a heartbeat like ours. Though it is very fast."

My heart sank.

"That is bad?"

Rika glanced at me, then back down.

"I do not know, my Gahn. It may be, it may not be. She is not like us."

Rika was worrying at Zeezee's clothing, her fingers finding a tiny little piece near the top that, when pulled, ran down the length of her cloak, peeling it away with an odd *zrrrrp* sound. She pulled the stiff fabric away, then reared back with a small gasp. My own eyes widened, and I hissed.

"Gahn, is this woman with child?"

Zeezee had breasts, clearly visible through the thin fabric of the grey clothing she wore beneath her cloak. Women of the Sea Sands only developed breasts during pregnancy, the flesh swelling to feed their cubs, before flattening back into hardened muscle when the cub was weaned.

"I do not know," I said truthfully, choosing my words carefully. "But I do not think so." It was unheard of that the Lavrika would choose a mate already with child for a warrior. I took a breath. "This woman is named Zeezee. She is my mate. I saw her face in the Lavrika Pools, more than fourteen days ago."

The air in the tent grew hushed. Rika was staring up at me, her gaze narrowed, the sight stars pulled to tiny bright points as she regarded me. Galok was gaping, first at me, then down at my mate. I did not like the hopeful sort of hunger I saw in his eyes when his gaze swept over her form, settling on her plump breasts. I snarled, my tail thrashing a warning at him, and he snapped to attention, his head jerking up.

"Both of you must go, now. I need to concentrate. Gahn Buroudei, is there any other information you think will help me?"

My mouth opened and shut, the sense of helplessness returning.

"No. None."

"Then go."

Galok headed out of the tent first, stealing one more glance backward as he did so. I began to leave, too, when I suddenly turned back, unable to take that final step out of the tent. I knelt next to Rika, grasping one of Zeezee's hands and pressing her tiny knuckles to my forehead. After a moment, I lowered her hand back down, carefully, so carefully, before turning my attention to Rika.

"Do not let her die."

There was a dangerous note of warning in my growl, but she held my gaze steadily.

"I will do what I can do."

I waited another moment before finally standing and turning to go, though everything in my body screamed at me to stay. But I could do nothing for my mate now. And that fact made me want to howl.

Galok was waiting for me outside of the tent. He was the tallest in our tribe, even taller than me. His long hair was unbound, flowing freely about his broad shoulders and back. He fell into step beside me as I stalked away from the healers' tent. I thought about going to join the evening fire, but decided against it. I had no desire to be around others now. Though, it seemed Galok was not planning to leave my side anytime soon.

"Buroudei, tell me more. Tell me everything you know of these females."

His voice was gruff with some unspoken desire. I could not blame him – with so few females, not just in our tribe, but all the surrounding ones, many warriors had resigned themselves to lives of companionless celibacy with no cubs. Suddenly, there was the chance that all of that could change.

I sighed, passing my hand roughly over my ears and hair. It was hard for me to converse with Galok now, hard for me to partake in his new hope when my own precious mate was listless on the healers' mats.

"It is as I told Rika. I have no other information for you, Galok."

"Come now, Buroudei. You are holding back. How many were there, and do they all look like her, your Zeezee?"

I cast my mind back to the chaotic scene on the sands.

"Maybe two dozen of them, though I'm not certain. And, from what I could see, only females. They are all somewhat similar but with wildly varying colouring. And different sizes."

"Do they all have breasts?" There was a boyish reverence in Galok's voice. We stopped walking at the outcropping of boulders, where the irkdu roamed. My own mount had joined its brethren and was chewing peet grass in the starlight.

"I do not know." The women all wore the same shapeless cloaks, hiding their figures. I hadn't even known my own mate had had such a feature.

"It is strange. A woman without a cub, but with breasts."

I cast a warning glance at my friend. Galok was my closest man, and as such, he could press further in conversation than any other. But even now, he was testing my limits. His sight stars were blown open, swirling, and his mouth was relaxed into a faraway sort of grin. When he caught my eye, he swallowed quickly, looking away. He vaulted forward, bounding up the side of the largest boulder, settling himself into a sitting position at the top.

"Come, Buroudei. You can do nothing for your mate right now, and something tells me if you were to return to your tent you would not sleep."

He was right about that. It had been a hard day of fighting and journeying over the sands. My body ached with exhaustion. And yet there was no chance that I'd be able to sleep now. I sprang up the craggy side of the boulder, sitting next to Galok, crossing my legs and placing my elbows on my knees. From here, we could see our spread of tents easily, and the fire with our kinsmen below. My eyes settled on the healers' tent and stayed there.

"So, Gahn Fallo has the others?"

"Yes."

"And what do you plan to do about that?"

"I have no real plan yet. But I do not intend to let him keep them."

I heard the grin in Galok's voice when he answered.

"That is what I was hoping to hear, friend."

He paused for a moment, his legs dangling over the side of the boulder, leaning back on his hands and looking up at the sky.

"You will have no trouble convincing the men to face Gahn Fallo if they are fighting for the chance at a potential mate."

I snorted.

"When have I ever had to convince any man of our tribe to do anything?"

I gave commands. And those commands were always followed without question.

"You are right. But you understand my meaning. Men will jump at the chance for one of the new women, even if it means facing zeelk or krixel or the spears of Gahn Fallo, whose men outnumber ours two-to-one. Especially since we can mate with them. The fact the Lavrika has chosen this woman for you is a momentous thing, my friend. I wish you the happiest of all lives, with many cubs."

A companionable warmth settled in my chest, and I placed one of my hands on Galok's shoulder and squeezed.

"I wish for the same thing. Assuming she survives the night."

The words were like poison in my mouth, but Galok just reached around and patted my back.

"I have no doubt that she will. Any mate of yours will have to have a will of ablik. She must be a strong one, to put up with you."

I frowned.

"And your mate will have to have enough sense for the both of you, to make up for the dakrival dung between your ears."

Galok's laugh was hearty, and it lessened the weight in my chest. Just a little.

We hadn't been there long, but my tail was beginning to twitch with impatient anxiety.

"I think I will return to the healers' tent. I want to check on Zeezee."

Galok clucked at me, the way a woman would cluck at a cub.

"Give Rika time. Your distractions will only hinder her."

He was right. But still I stood, jumping down to the sand in one great leap. Galok followed immediately, landing with powerful grace beside me.

"I will not distract Rika. But I cannot be away from Zeezee any longer. It's like this pull, Galok. This pull that will not let me rest in any one place without her."

Galok was looking at me strangely, and I waved him off.

"Nevermind. You cannot understand without a mate."

Galok's face hardened.

"You are right. I have no mate and cannot understand."

Curse me twenty thousand times. I was far more stupid than usual tonight. I placed my hand on his shoulder once again.

"I am sorry, friend. I did not mean it that way. I am sick with worry and longing. It is new and strange and it is making my head foggy. About you not having a mate – well, we will rectify that soon enough. You are the most deserving of men, strong and loyal and battle-hardened. I have no doubt the Lavrika will come to you soon. And we will take your precious mate, along with the others, back from Gahn Fallo."

Galok watched me for a moment, his sight stars pulled tight, before they unspooled and he relaxed again. He clasped my elbow, his face resolute.

"Thank you, Buroudei."

We began walking back towards the tents.

"May I tell the others what you've told me?"

I mulled on the question. Everyone would find out eventually when they caught a glimpse of Zeezee. There was no reason to hide it, now.

"Yes. Go head and share the news." It would be good to give the people of the tribe something to celebrate. New women, new blood, new cubs to be born. The men would feast with renewed vigour tonight. But my smile at the thought was only a shadow. I was too consumed with worry for Zeezee to partake in the excitement.

Galok bounded towards the evening fire, and I turned back towards the healers' tent. I did not go inside, though I longed to do so, instead crouching down on the sand outside.

I would station myself here for the night. And every other night, if needed. Still as a desert boulder, I waited, my heart the only thing moving.

And it did not just move.

It thundered.

CHAPTER NINE
Cece

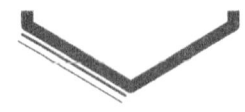

The first thing I became aware of was a dull throbbing in my head. Then a thick dryness in my mouth. I groaned, licking my lips with a heavy tongue, and opened my eyes. I was in some kind of large canopied area, or maybe a tent, but a big one with a flat roof, more like a fabric gazebo. I stared up at the light brown fabric of the roof, dazed, as firelight flickered from somewhere nearby. It took me a long moment to remember where I was.

But it all came crashing back when I heard someone, or something, speak beside me. My head jerked to the side, and I gasped at the sight of another alien. But this one wasn't my alien. *Hold on. My alien?* This one seemed older, at least by human standards, with a long white braid, and eyes with silver sparks. They wore a simple woven covering, like a tunic, belted with the same kind of leathery fabric that Buroudei had had crossed across his body.

"Where's Buroudei?" I asked, latching onto the one alien who was somewhat familiar to me on this world. An alien I inexplicably thought of as "my alien."

At his name the other alien seemed to react, their eyes glittering. They said something else. Their voice seemed higher and softer than Buroudei's, but still a little growly. And there was a softness to the features. That, coupled with the different garb, convinced me this must be one of the female aliens. *Maybe he took me home and dumped me off with his mom.*

She said something else, then pointed a knobby, clawed finger at my legs. Gingerly, I sat up and pulled back the animal hide blanket that had been tucked around me. Heat flooded my cheeks and neck as I realized I was naked, and I yanked the blanket back, clutching it around my chest. The alien cocked her head, said something else, and gestured to my legs again. Blushing fiercely, I pulled the blanket up a bit and looked down again.

My inner thighs had been bandaged with some kind of lightweight woven fabric. I poked at them, flinching, expecting pain, but there was none, besides a little stiffness. I didn't seem to be bleeding anymore, either. I tugged at the edge of a bandage, and gasped. My skin was shiny and pink and freshly healed. *How long was I asleep for? A week? Two weeks?*

But I didn't feel hungry or weak enough to have been out that long. It made no damn sense.

The alien woman seemed to understand my confusion. She said more, and then picked up a small clay jar, taking off the lid and holding it out to me. I was suspicious for a moment, but then again, she had apparently healed me with some kind of alien sorcery, so it didn't seem like she would hurt me now. I glanced inside the jar.

The jar looked like it was filled with radioactive milk. Thick and white, the liquid glowed as it swirled in the jar. The alien pulled the jar back, mimicking dipping her fingers in it, then rubbing the insides of her thighs. *Ah. So this stuff is some kind of Polysporin on steroids. Got it.* Whatever it was, I was grateful – the pain in my legs from before was basically gone, and the number one thing bothering me now was a pounding head and dry throat.

"Do you have any water?"

She looked at me blankly.

I mimed drinking from a cup, then pointed to my throat.

"Thirsty. Need water."

A look of understanding crossed her features, and she stood, crossing to the other side of the tent and fetching one of those spiky cacti that Buroudei had shown me earlier. *Valok.* She grabbed a small, sharp instrument from a nearby shelf, and sliced the valok the way Buroudei had, pulling it open and offering it to me.

I bit my lip. Was this safe? It didn't seem like such a bright idea. But then again, if they had no water, I was done for either way. I might as well give this a shot. Who knew how far I was from the ship and our supplies. Taking a steadying breath, I grabbed the valok plant and slurped some of the innards out.

I coughed a bit as I swallowed. The stuff was more bitter than I'd anticipated. Like green tea that had been left to steep too long. But as far as I could tell, that was the worst of it. After a moment, when nothing in my body seemed to rebel against it, I took my chances and half-drank, half-ate some more of the slippery gel. By the time I'd mostly emptied the round valok plant, I felt surprisingly better. It had slaked my thirst, and my headache was already abating. *Damn, between the magic aloe plants and the radioactive milk, these guys have got medicine surprisingly well figured out.*

The tall alien woman looked satisfied, and took the valok husk from my hands, disposing of it in a corner and grabbing something else. When she brought it closer, I realized it was some kind of plate, carved from bone, filled with what appeared to be meat.

My stomach simultaneously flip-flopped and grumbled. I was hungry, no doubt about that, but I wasn't sure I was quite hungry enough to eat whatever that was. But she nudged it toward me with greater urgency, speaking quickly. I could practically hear my Grammy speaking through her, telling me to eat my meat and vegetables so that I'd have lots of energy and strength. *I guess grandmas getting young people to eat is universal. Literally.*

The thought made me soften, and I took the plate, casting my eyes over it to find something that looked somewhat edible. I steered clear of what appeared to be raw organ meat, and settled on something that resembled sliced beef, lightly charred.

I took a bite. The flavour was strong and gamy, and it was extremely tough to chew. But all in all, it was palatable. I spent a few moments chowing down, sure that I looked absolutely crazy – naked in an alien tent, eating a bunch of meat with my bare hands. But with every bite I swallowed I felt stronger. When I'd had enough, I handed the plate back to the woman. She took it, standing, then disappeared outside of the tent.

I sighed contentedly, or as contentedly as I could, considering the situation. Sure, I'd been dropped by my own people on an alien planet, had barely survived some kind of spider apocalypse, but I was also feeling about a hundred times better than I had been earlier, and I seemed to have made some new friends. Or, at least, allies of some kind. I hoped.

A second later, I heard the tent fabric rustle, and I turned towards the sound, expecting to see the alien woman return. But it wasn't her. I bit back a gasp, yanking the blankets I'd let slip back up to my shoulders.

No, this definitely wasn't the woman from before. This alien was tall, insanely muscled, and was staring at me like I was a piece of raw meat on a plate.

It was Buroudei.

With the half-crazed look of hunger on his face, I almost expected he'd bound over and take a massive bite out of my arm. But he didn't. He crossed the space between us with a few long strides. His tail whipped around his front, covering his eyes, then he knelt, his tail returning behind him. He grabbed for my hands, holding them tightly, almost reverently. Laughing awkwardly, I yanked one hand back to keep my blanket in place in front of my torso.

"Nice to see you again, too. Thanks for getting me here and all patched up. Was that your mom?"

I gestured out the way the woman had left. He cocked his head for a moment, then said a bunch of words. I only caught the last syllables, which he repeated.

"Rika." He pointed the way the woman had left, saying, "Rika," then pointing to himself and saying, "Buroudei."

"Right, got it. Don't worry, I didn't forget your name, Buroudei."

When I said his name, the shimmering speckles in his eyes exploded outwards, and he gave a guttural sounding groan, his mouth descending to my hand that he still held. And there was that batshit crazy tongue again, long and forked into three parts, working its way over my palm. When he reached the sensitive skin of my wrist I choked back a cry. This felt way too good. Was this some kind of alien greeting I didn't understand? He'd done it before, to my neck. In all the footage we'd studied, I hadn't seen an alien lick another one upon meeting them. And, for some reason, the idea of Buroudei's tongue going to town on somebody else just felt... wrong.

Holy shit, girl. Are you jealous?

Between intense licks, Buroudei was muttering away, his dark eyes never leaving mine. I couldn't understand a single word coming out of his terrifying mouth, but something in his tone felt like he was telling me something important. Making some kind of promise. I only wished I knew what it was.

I stared at him as he moved fervently to my inner elbow. His features were strange, absolutely, but there was a feral beauty to them. Not to mention the god-like physique – the broad frame, the tight ripple of muscles. Sure, his ears and claws and tail and *tongues* may have been weird as hell, but somehow it all worked, creating a brutal, strong, entirely-too-enticing image. Heat sparked beneath my skin everywhere he licked, travelling up my arm, pooling in my abdomen before moving deep into my pelvis. Something deep and primal was responding to his touch. Something terrifying and new that I wasn't so sure I could control.

Oh, *God,* I was getting horny for an alien.

I always knew my crush on the fox in Robin Hood would come back to bite me in the ass.

I clenched my newly healed thighs together, and Buroudei reared back, snarling something before whipping the blanket up and away from my legs.

"Excuse *me,*" I cried, frantically pulling the blanket back to cover my naked crotch. But Buroudei wasn't looking there. He was examining my bandaged legs closely. He reached one clawed finger towards the edge of a bandage, then pulled back, his face clenching in what looked like dark pain. His voice, when he spoke, was like shattering steel.

"If you're asking how I am, well, Rika fixed me right up."

I tugged at the edge of the bandages, revealing a strip of the shiny pink skin.

"See?"

Buroudei did see. He was seeing a little too much, perhaps. Because he was frozen in place, every muscle tight with tension as his pulsing gaze travelled up my thighs to their junction, barely covered with my crumpled blanket. My breath caught in my throat as I watched him watching me.

And then he descended with a guttural sound, his tongue working at the pink skin I'd just shown him. At the same time, his huge hands reached up, gripping my hips as I gasped. His fangs brushed my skin and I cried out, sparks zinging up to my pussy.

Is this fucked up? Is this wrong?

It probably was. But in that moment, I didn't give two flying fucks. For the first time since I'd lost Grammy, I didn't feel alone. And, frankly, the past few weeks had been all kinds of messed up. Could anyone blame me for going a little nuts right now? For letting this happen? For wanting this?

I let my legs fall open.

Hunger radiated off of Buroudei in massive waves, slamming through me, twanging deep in my core. He skimmed over the bandaged surface of my inner thighs, his face settling between my legs. He breathed in, deeply, then nosed my curls, groaning. He dragged his nose up and down my folds, folds grown slick with totally messed up and totally inescapable desire. I felt like I'd descended into some kind of fever dream.

And as his tongue found its way to my aching entrance, I knew that I did not want to wake up.

CHAPTER TEN
Buroudei

If I'd thought Zeezee's blood was sweet, it was nothing, *nothing*, compared to this. This was nectar, ambrosia, more fulfilling and sustaining than sacred Lavrika's blood. I fervently thanked my long-dead parents for giving me three strong tongues, and simultaneously wished that I had more. More tongues, more mouths, more hands. I wanted every part of myself against every part of my strange new mate.

This was a hunger unlike any I'd ever felt before. Laying with Zanixia paled in comparison to this, this clawing desire, this desperate need. This addiction.

The centre part of my tongue circled Zeezee's slick entrance while the outer parts tracked through incredibly soft folds of skin. Folds that were, strangely and beautifully, surrounded by dark hair. It was shocking, and erotic beyond measure, to find hair there. I groaned as I breathed deep of her musk, the scent and taste of her rocking through my body, sending my cock into painful hardness.

I moved up slightly, the centre tongue encountering a taut nub of flesh that, when tasted, made Zeezee cry out. Her back arched, her hips almost coming right off the bedding. I growled, watching her, continuing to explore that small nub, her wetness coating my lips and chin. This seemed to give her great pleasure, her voice tremulous as she made little moaning sounds. For women of the Sea Sands, all their pleasure points were inside their cunts. To have this exposed bit of flesh that was so sensitive, so vulnerable to my tongue, inflamed me. I liked how easily it made her come undone. I slicked back and forth over it, the outer segments of my tongue coming up to stroke along the sides. Zeezee still clutched the dakrival hide blanket to her chest, and I bit back a growl of irritation at the sight, redoubling my tongues' efforts. *I will bring her so much pleasure that she is incapable of hiding her body from me. She will bare every naked morsel of perfect flesh in ecstasy by the time I am finished, and she will beg me to mate her.*

She was saying something now, panting, the words like nonsense in my ears, but beautiful nonsense, because they were hers. Her face was flushed with a surprising shade of red, her pink lips parted, her bright eyes wide as she looked down at me. My cock throbbed as my grip shifted, my thumbs coming to rest on her inner thighs, right at her groin, forcing her legs wider apart. I kept the centre part of my tongue locked against that little nub of pleasure, while the outer parts moved back down, probing at her soaked entrance. The thought of my cock pressing against that wet heat almost made me lose control, almost had me lose my seed without a single stroke against my hardness. I fought back the waves of need building inside me, focusing only on my tongue, and Zeezee's delicious heat.

Zeezee was saying something that sounded a lot like ahfak, our word for morning sun. I knew that wasn't what she meant, but the image was a good one – the cresting of heat and light, the bursting of brightness in darkness. Zeezee was cresting, now, her hips rolling, her odd, lovely eyes scrunched shut, her head thrown back. I watched her in hungry fascination, taking in each moan, each toss of her head, each quiver of her thighs. My pride (alongside my cock) swelled when my prediction came true: as she reached the height of her pleasure, arching her hips right up off the ground and screaming, she forgot all about the dakrival hide clutched to her chest and let it fall, revealing a smooth, soft abdomen and rounded white breasts with taut pink tips. I eyed those pink, soft nipples, pulled to tight points, feverishly. *That is the next place my mouth will explore.*

Zeezee let loose another string of nonsense sounds, then, but there was no mistaking the one word that came at the very end. Because it was my name. My name was what left her lips as she reached the peak of her pleasure.

Everything inside me raged. Not being inside her was unadulterated agony.

So this is the power of the sacred mate bond.

It felt like it was destroying me and making me whole, all at once.

I moved up to my knees with a choked-back snarl, one of my hands remaining possessively on Zeezee's hip while my other deftly pulled off my loincloth, letting my hardness spring free. Though I knew she would not understand, I spoke anyway.

"I have waited years for you, my Zeezee. Years upon years of aching for someone I did not know existed. And now that you are here you are everything and more. You are strange. And you are perfect. And you are mine."

Zeezee opened her eyes as I spoke, looking at me, dazed. But when her gaze fell to my cock, her small mouth dropped open and her eyes seemed to focus instantly. And then she started shaking her head back and forth, the way she had earlier, the way she had when she was unhappy.

"Nononononono."

There was no mistaking the meaning of her foreign words. And in case I had mistaken it, she reinforced it with the yanking of the dakrival hide over her beautiful breasts, and the tossing up of a hand between us, as if it were a wall. A tiny, soft wall that I could topple with the flick of a finger. But a wall all the same.

My chest clenched, and I moved my hands to the sides of her face, staring into her wide eyes.

"Why do you refuse me?"

She did not get the chance to answer in her unknown language. Because at that moment, my ears twitched at the sound of irkdu moving across the sands towards our tents, and the calling of strange voices, answered by the angry shouts of my men. I heard the unsheathing of weapons, and immediately I stood, returning my loincloth to my body and turning from Zeezee. This conversation, if one could even call it that, would have to wait. If enemy warriors were approaching, then Zeezee, along with everyone in the tribe, could be in danger. A dark wave broke over me.

Perhaps Gahn Fallo has come back to claim the one woman his men did not retrieve.

The thought turned to molten ablik in my guts, burning then hardening everything.

Let him try to take my Zeezee. I'll set Zaphrinax on fire, burn it all to the ground, before I let her go.

I spoke quickly, pulling two of my knives from the straps at my back.

"Stay still and quiet. I will return for you. Do not come out."

Zeezee's brows crumpled inwards in confusion, but I had no time to try to explain further. Enemies were circling us, even now.

I bounded out of the tent, knives tight in my grip, and the taste of Zeezee on my lips.

⟨ ⟩

I RUSHED THROUGH THE tents towards the sounds. The evening fire was in my sights, and I could see the women dispersing quickly, pulling their cubs along with them. My warriors were gathered on the other side of the fire, looking out towards the sand, spears and knives and axes brandished and ready, waiting for my command. Galok was sprinting towards me, but he stopped when he saw that I had heard the commotion and was coming on my own. I caught up to him quickly, and we ran together around the fire, out past the tents, followed by the rest of my warriors.

"It's Gahn Irokai," Galok informed me as we stopped running, standing with our weapons ready. This surprised me. Gahn Irokai's territory was days from here, at the base of the mountains at the very edge of the Sea Sands. Our territories did not border each other and we had no current cause for quarrel – no wars over land or resources had been fought between our two tribes in generations. I had been sure that this was Gahn Fallo, whose territory was nearest ours and whose men we often fought with. My warriors were shouting, showcasing their fangs and their blades as we watched the small group approach. I stared at the dark shadows of the intruders. It was a small party, like a hunting party. It was not the full force of Gahn Irokai's men.

Gahn Irokai's booming voice rose over the warning growls of my men. "Gahn Buroudei! I do not come in war. I ask safe passage into your tent. I must have words with you."

My men stilled, watching me silently, waiting for me to make a decision. Any warrior who rose to the role of Gahn was mighty, and was to be treated as a threat. But the people of the Sea Sands were not usually deceptive. If Gahn Irokai was here for battle, he and his men would be charging at us with war cries, blades already flying. But they approached calmly, no weapons drawn. I stepped forward, sheathing my weapons, but keeping my eye trained on him and his men and irkdu.

There were only five of them. At the head, riding the largest irkdu, was Gahn Irokai, and at his side was his best warrior, whom I recognized as Taliok. I did not know the names of the others.

When they were within a spear's throwing distance, Gahn Irokai and Taliok dismounted, followed soon by the others, crossing the last distance towards us on foot. Gahn Irokai hulked, his hair greying, but his eyes just as sharp as ever. Taliok strode next to him, a dark expression on his scarred face. They both raised their tails in respectful greeting, which surprised me and put me a little more at ease. I did the same, grunting, and my men followed suit.

I turned to two of the warriors standing just behind me, Malachor and Rawk.

"Take their irkdu to the peet grass between the boulders. Stay with the beasts and keep them from fighting." Our irkdu were well trained, but, like their masters, were naturally territorial. They could easily be moved to aggression by the scent of these new animals. Malachor and Rawk raised their tails in acknowledgement, then led the creatures away from us, out towards the boulders. Gahn Irokai nodded at two of his men to accompany them, then approached, coming to a stop before me, flanked by Taliok and one other warrior.

"You see I have come with few warriors, and have not drawn weapons."

I twitched my tail in understanding.

"I do. You and your men will not be harmed here tonight." I paused, then continued, a slight growl colouring my voice. "But you should know that if you make a single threat, I will not stop my men and irkdu from tearing your party limb from limb."

Gahn Irokai grunted. "As it should be among Gahns."

We walked back around the fire, moving through the tents towards my own tent, the second largest after the healers' tents. Gahn Irokai and I walked side by side, followed by Galok, Taliok, and Gahn Irokai's third warrior. I heard the warrior tell Galok his name was Oxriel as we walked.

I kept my gaze firmly trained on Gahn Irokai from the corner of my eye. True to his word, he did not seem to be here for violent purposes. But I would not let my guard down yet. Especially when I now had something so precious to protect.

Even with this surprise, and the significance of receiving another Gahn here tonight, my mind kept moving back to Zeezee. With a jolt,

I stopped, calling to a nearby group of warriors who had dispersed towards the fire after the threat had been gauged.

"Teelk and Vaxilkai, go and guard the healers' tent. Make sure no one goes in. Or out."

They knew better than to hesitate, but I saw the flash of confusion in their eyes as they moved to execute my order. Perhaps Galok had not yet told them about the news of Zeezee and the other women. *I will have to ask him about that later.*

We reached my tent. Galok pulled aside the hide for Gahn Irokai and me, and we moved inside, followed by the other three warriors. Inside, Galok lit two valok candles, placing them on either side of my seat, a large dakrival hide stool stuffed with peet grass and stones to make it firm and heavy.

"I do not have a seat for you, Gahn Irokai," I said, noting the single stool. I had never needed a second one before. No other Gahn had ever come here in peace during my lifetime.

"A Gahn is not afraid of being seated on the sand like his people."

I approved of this, and we all sat on the sand, Galok and I facing the three of them.

"Will you and your men take meat and valok? We were feasting when you arrived. I know it is a long journey from your mountains."

Gahn Irokai moved his hand through the air.

"No. Not yet. Afterwards we will partake of your hospitality. But what I have to tell is too important to wait."

My ears pricked, and I noticed Galok lean forward. Neither of us could ignore the fact that this was happening the day the new women had arrived. It could be no coincidence.

"I want to call a meeting of the Gahns."

I heard Galok hiss in surprise next to me, but I kept my countenance calm. A meeting of the Gahns had not been called in many generations. Not since our population had begun to die off due to the actions of our ancestors. Our ancestors who had ignored the sacred Lavrika's call. Meetings of the Gahns involved calling together all five Gahns of the Sea Sands. Historically, they either resulted in new pacts and alliances or ended in utter bloodshed.

"Why?"

I had a feeling I knew what could have disturbed Gahn Irokai so much as to require a meeting of the Gahns. It had to be related to Zeezee's people. I felt a muscle twitch at the base of my tail. I longed to go to her, even now. To check on her, make sure she was safe.

Though Gahn Irokai had seemed to be in a rush before, now that it was time to explain himself, he faltered, taking several deep breaths then halting before speaking. Finally, he said, "It will be better if Taliok speaks to our purpose, if you will hear him."

"This is agreeable," I muttered, shifting my focus to the brooding young warrior.

Taliok did not move to speak, his jaw drawn tight. But a grunt from his Gahn shifted him to action. His voice was low and dark.

"Some days ago the Lavrika called me to the pools."

I tensed, and felt Galok's tail twitch.

"The mate I saw there was like no woman of the Sea Sands. Like no creature of Zaphrinax. She had no tail, no claws, and terrible white eyes."

So it was as I had thought. It was to do with the new women. I hadn't known one of Gahn Irokai's men had travelled to the pools. The Cliffs of Uruzai were considered neutral territory, accessible to all the people of the Sea Sands. Much of the open sands between the mountains and the cliffs were also neutral territory – too dangerous and barren to bother fighting to claim. My patrolling parties would not have seen Taliok come that way, and would not have bothered him on the way to the Cliffs, anyway. I waited in silence, absorbing this information and allowing Taliok more time to speak if he had more to say. But it appeared he did not. He lapsed back into frowning silence.

I mulled this over as everyone watched me. Did I admit everything now? That I, too, had seen, and had now found, my strange mate? There would be instant suspicion at the fact that I had not tried to call a meeting of the Gahns the way Irokai had. I suddenly thought back to my warriors' confusion at my order to guard the healers' tent, indicating that Galok had not shared the news of the new women yet. *It seems we both want to keep these small and precious creatures to ourselves.*

But such a thing would be impossible, now. Perhaps even now the men of the other tribes were seeing their mates in the Lavrika Pools.

This complicates things.

I would have to tell Gahn Irokai everything. Start to finish. *At least now I have a potential ally to take the other women back from Gahn Fallo. If his closest man has a mate among them, Gahn Irokai will no doubt lend warriors to our purpose.* I opened my mouth to speak, to tell him of my own pretty mate, when a sudden commotion crashed outside. Warriors were shouting, and then came a sound so bright and sharp it burned: the scream of my mate.

I was up and moving instantly, my guests forgotten. I was only slightly aware of Gahn Irokai asking me something and Taliok jumping up and drawing his weapons. They would have to wait. They would all have to wait until I made sure my Zeezee was alright.

Outside, a group of warriors had gathered in a circle. At the centre was one of the warriors I'd assigned to the healers' tent, Teelk. One of his arms held Zeezee firmly against his body. The other held a blade to her throat.

I was not known as a rash or vicious Gahn. Brutal in battle, yes, and a fierce warrior. But I was not insane, not like Gahn Fallo. In that moment, though, seeing that blade against Zeezee's incredible skin, her slender pulsing throat, I felt all sanity slip away. A sky-tearing cry exploded from my chest, and then I was running, men parting before me in confused terror at my rage. Galok shouted something from behind me, but I ignored him, yanking a blade from my back. Teelk stood stock still, frozen in confusion, as Zeezee kicked and fought his embrace. This was one of my men, one of my own warriors. And in that moment I did not care. His hands on her, his weapon at her neck, made me so sick with black anger that I was ready to tear him apart. I raised my blade, snarling -

- only to have it knocked away by another blade. I whirled, finding Taliok in my way.

Gahn Irokai broke into the circle, calling to his man. "Taliok, answer me now. Is this the female you saw in the pools? Is this your mate?"

I could have taken Taliok's life for the disrespect he'd just shown me, and I bared my fangs, raising my blade again. My warriors gnashed their teeth, drawing their own weapons. Gahn Irokai and his men had come in peace, but they would leave covered in blood.

At that moment, Zeezee gave a small cry, managing to wriggle out of Teelk's arms, his grip grown slack with confusion and shock. She ran to me, *to me*, her soft body colliding against mine, her arms wrapping around my waist. I clutched her protectively against my side, holding my knife up against Taliok. Taliok's sight stars drew in to focused points as he stared at us, his gaze moving back and forth between my face and Zeezee's. After a tense moment, he sheathed his blade.

He answered Gahn Irokai. "Now that I see her closer, I know she is not my mate. But she is of the same people." Then he spoke to me. "I thought you drew your blade to harm her. That you saw her as an enemy."

"She is no enemy," I growled, pulling her tighter.

It was time. The news could wait no longer.

"She is my mate."

CHAPTER ELEVEN
Cece

Can someone please explain how I have ended up here?

OK, I knew how I'd ended up grabbed by yet another alien gladiator-looking dude. At least, sort of. The guy had been assigned to watch me, clearly. And clearly, I hadn't been as stealthy as I had thought, sneaking out of the other side of the tent.

Yeah, it probably wasn't a great idea to try to leave the tent. But what choice did I have? Just sit there like some princess in a tower waiting for my hunky alien with *three fucking tongues* to come back and bed me? No way. I'd seen that monster cock. That was not going to happen.

I'd stayed in the tent a long time after Buroudei had left, partly in shock, and partly because I was pretty sure I'd never walk again after that orgasm. I was in shock that it had even happened, for one thing, and that he had left so quickly afterwards. At some point, though, my curiosity got the better of me, and I knew I couldn't stay there anymore. Not to mention the fact that I still needed to try to get back to the wreckage for supplies, and try, somehow, to find my friends. If there was anything left of them.

My clothes were stiff with dried blood and sweat, but Rika had left a tunic-like garment, similar to the one she'd worn, by my bed. I'd put it on, and had had to hold back a laugh at how insanely huge it was on me. This species sure wasn't lacking in the height department. *Or girth.* Oh, God.

When I'd crept to the main flap of the tent I'd seen the two hulking warrior dudes waiting right outside, armed to the teeth. Or, fangs, in this case. There was no way I would have made it out that way. So I'd gone back to the other side, pulling up at one of the walls of the tent and crawling out under it, burrowing through the sand as I did so. I didn't know if they heard me or smelled me or what, but I'd only made it a little ways before one of them yelped a warning, and the other one had caught up to me in about two seconds flat.

And that was how I'd ended up here, screaming my head off as yet another alien refused to let me go.

But this felt different. This wasn't my alien. This wasn't the one I knew. The one I sort of trusted now. The one I maybe kind of actually liked. And when this alien's gigantic blade came up to hover under my chin, I felt the difference between them keenly.

Other alien men were gathering around us now, staring and calling out as I fought my captor.

"Fuck you, and fuck your fucking stupid sword," I screamed, wriggling and kicking, trying to do anything to get out of this embrace. The alien holding me said something, gripping me tighter, and the others watching moved closer.

I didn't like the look of this. At all. Buroudei was nowhere to be seen, and I didn't trust any of these new guys as far as I couldn't throw them. Which, considering their impressive weight to my paltry upper body strength, was saying something.

Did I really survive getting abducted on Earth, space travel, and an insane crab attack, only to get snuffed out here, now? It couldn't be true. Although, I was somewhat heartened to notice that the guy holding me didn't seem like he was exactly itching to use his weapon on me. He was swinging his head around above me, as if looking for someone. *Waiting for instructions?*

And then I heard it. An alien howl, primal and furious and powerful beyond measure. Goosebumps exploded over my skin, my hair standing on end at the sound. Suddenly the men standing around watching were practically falling over themselves to get out of the way of something.

Or someone.

Buroudei.

I never thought I'd be so fucking happy to see my alien tyrant. The one who'd kidnapped me. Who'd saved me. Who'd made me come so hard I'd seen stars. Clearly, I wasn't the only one who thought he was a tyrant – Buroudei was hauling ass, and the other men were basically jumping out of his way. The guy holding me had frozen totally still in submissive fear. To be honest, I was a little scared, too. Buroudei was almost unrecognizable as he hurtled towards us, his face viciously dark, his blade high in the air, about to strike.

Before he could reach us, another alien stepped in, so quick and smooth it was like water. I had no idea where he came from, but suddenly there he was, with his own impressive weapon and a deeply scarred face, knocking Buroudei's blade to the side. I felt my chest lurch in sick fear, not for myself, but for Buroudei. I didn't know who this other guy was, but he seemed dangerous. I was pretty certain Buroudei could hold his own, but the thought of him getting hurt, or maybe even dying, was absolutely heart-rending. Which was absurd, considering I'd basically just met the guy. But there it was.

Rapid conversations were happening all around me, words I longed to understand. An impressively tall, older-looking alien spoke, his gruff voice authoritative, and the scarred alien responded. Buroudei looked like he was about to tear the scarred guy's head off. *I need to defuse this. I need to get to him.* I couldn't help but feel that I had somehow caused all this by leaving the tent, even though it had felt like my only option.

In the confusion, my captor's grip had slackened, and it gave me the chance I needed to slip out from his arms. I raced to Buroudei, clamping onto him with the ferocity of an angry toddler. I had no clue what that would accomplish – I wasn't exactly keen on the idea of being used as a human shield, but I just knew I had to be with him now. His arm immediately pulled me in, and once again I was struck by how different Buroudei felt to the other alien who had held me. There was a familiarity with him, a warmth beneath the hardness, a seductive sort of safety. I burrowed in closer.

The scarred alien was staring at us intensely. Then he put his weapon away, and I let out a tiny squeak of relief. He said something to Buroudei, and Buroudei responded, his voice a deep rumble that I felt in his chest.

Whatever Buroudei said, it must have been a bombshell. Gasps and tongue clicks of surprise ran through the group, and the scarred warrior's eye glimmers exploded outward, pulsing. The tall, older alien approached us, speaking rapidly, and I felt Buroudei's tail thrashing behind us in the sand. They were all looking at me.

Guess it's time to introduce myself.

I cleared my throat.

"Um. Hello. I'm Cece. From Earth."

The older alien reared back, and the scarred one's jaw worked furiously, his expression hard and twisting. Buroudei said something else, gesturing at a large tent, and after a long moment, the scarred alien and the older one, along with a few others, headed towards it as the rest of the men dispersed. Buroudei seemed like he would follow, but then his hands were on me – my hips, my waist, my neck, my jaw. He lowered his forehead to mine, saying something dark and quiet and sweet-sounding, and without thinking I raised my hands to his shoulders. God, his shoulders were huge, the muscles hard as stone. Barbarous male energy radiated off of every inch of him, and it was kind of... doing something to me. I couldn't lie – seeing him barrelling towards us, weapon raised, ready to defend me at all costs, had been weirdly enticing. I knew I was strong and didn't need rescuing. That I could take care of myself. At least, that was how it had been on Earth. That's what Grammy had always told me. But since I'd been abducted, all bets were off in that department. And, frankly, it felt good to have someone on my side, someone who, for some reason, seemed hellbent on protecting me. Even if that someone was now sporting a raging erection.

Heat slammed through me. Something about repeatedly almost dying on this God-forsaken planet was leaving me feeling weird, almost drunk. My inhibitions were fading fast.

"I'm glad you're OK," I whispered, my face still turned up to Buroudei's. He was bent to me, our faces so close that I could count each coppery spark in his alien eyes. My gaze fell to his mouth, then, and I realized I wanted to kiss him. *Do aliens even kiss?* Whatever. We'd make it work.

Slowly, so slowly, I raised myself on tiptoe and moved my mouth to his.

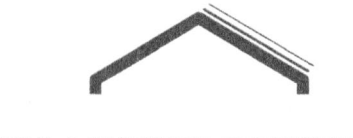

CHAPTER TWELVE
Buroudei

My mate was certainly prone to surprising me. Including now, by pressing her mouth to mine. It caught me off guard, and I remained still, waiting to see what else she would do, every muscle thrumming. My hands were like stone against her jaw, and I had to fight to remain gentle, reminding myself that I could crush her if I was not careful.

She made a small sound, her lips softening and parting against mine, her soft wet tongue poking out against my mouth, trying to work its way in. I let her have her way, opening my mouth slightly. She sighed against me – *steady, Buroudei, steady* – and her single tongue met my three. I felt a shiver run through her body, and my cock pulsed with insistent need against her abdomen.

The people of the Sea Sands used their mouths in all sorts of ways to create pleasure. But this, this pressing of one mouth to another, was usually reserved for mates. It was the first time I had done such a thing with a female. It felt even more intimate than my tongues at her cunt. But it was just as sweet. I felt her make little gasps as the three tips of my tongue brushed hers, working their way into her welcoming mouth, running along her blunt teeth. My tongue in her mouth reminded me of a cock in a cunt, and the image inflamed me. I had to pull myself away, then, my thumb brushing her wet lower lip.

"If I did not have another Gahn and his men waiting for me at my tent, I would have to take you right here on the sands."

She muttered a long string of her lilting words. And for a moment, I was totally bereft at not understanding her. An ache opened up in my chest, and without thinking I grasped one of her small hands, placing it on my skin, right above that ache.

"Feel this," I hissed, and her big eyes grew even bigger. If we could not communicate with words, I would find another way. I would make her feel me. My heart thundered beneath my skin, beneath her hand. "Feel this. This is for you. This is *yours*."

She did not yet know what it meant to have the heart of a Gahn. But she would learn.

I heard my name, and though I wished it were coming from Zeezee's lips, it was not. It was Galok, calling me from my tent where the others waited. I adjusted my loincloth, trying to ease some of my discomfort there. I pulled Zeezee's hand from my chest and held it carefully, leading her forward. For once, she followed and did not fight me. But I did not know if that was bad or good.

We reached my tent, and Galok tried to hide how much he stared, though he failed miserably. This was the first time he had seen Zeezee awake and moving. He held my tent's flap open for us, his eyes lingering on Zeezee's face as she ducked under his arm. A warning growl grew in my throat as I watched him sniff the air as she passed. He ducked his head, whipping his tail up over his eyes in apology. The tent flap fell closed as we all moved in.

Taliok, Oxriel, and Gahn Irokai were standing, facing us. Their weapons were sheathed, but the tension in their bodies was clear. They were ready to fight if needed. The uneasy decorum from earlier had evaporated, leaving only danger and mistrust. I held Zeezee protectively at my side. I had thought about sending her back to the healers' tent, with more guards this time, but that wouldn't do. Not now that they had seen her. Besides, I didn't trust anyone in my tribe to keep her safe but me. I would not let her leave my side.

"Gahn Buroudei. I demand an explanation." Gahn Irokai's voice was gruff but mostly level. Yet I understood the threat there, beneath the calm surface. Though he and his men were greatly outnumbered, they could do bloody battle with us and still cause significant damage to the tribe. But he was right. He needed to understand what was going on. Now that Zeezee was pressed tight to my side, the animosity from earlier had dissipated, and my usually clear head was returning.

"I will explain. And I will forgive your man Taliok's disrespect earlier, when he crossed blades with me."

Gahn Irokai's tail moved in satisfaction, but Taliok grunted.

"I thought she was my mate. I thought you were going to kill her."

I bit back a bark of irritation.

"You need to learn to watch your tongues around another Gahn."

Gahn Irokai tensed, and Taliok's hand moved, ever so slightly, towards the long blade at his belt. Galok shifted into a defensive stance. Every instinct in me screamed to defend myself and my tribe and my territory and destroy the men before me. My lip curled back from my fangs.

Just then, Zeezee shifted against me, drawing in closer, sensing the tension. I forced my pride down, something I was not accustomed to. But I did it for her. I would not have her at the centre of this bloodshed. I breathed out, and the others visibly relaxed.

"If you thought she was your mate I can understand your reaction. As I said before, I am willing to overlook it now."

Gahn Irokai glanced at silent Taliok, then back at me.

"Very well," he said.

I told them everything I knew. I told them how the Lavrika had come to me, just as it had come to Taliok. I told them how today, a great creature had fallen from the sky, spilling women from its belly. And I told them that Zeezee was the only female here, the rest of them taken by Gahn Fallo. At those lasts words, Taliok hissed, turning to pace the length of the tent as I finished speaking.

"That is everything. All I know."

Gahn Irokai watched me for a long moment.

"I believe you."

"Good. Because it is the truth."

The other Gahn raked his claws over his braid.

"Taliok, stop that incessant pacing. I cannot think."

Taliok's tail thrashed, but he slowed, coming to a stop next to Oxriel. His hand was tight on the hilt of his blade, but that caused me no concern. I knew that he was picturing using that weapon on Gahn Fallo, now. Not me.

"I do not think a meeting of the Gahns is prudent now. I do not think Gahn Fallo would agree to go or agree to give up the women. Especially if any of them are mates to his men. If he knows our people can mate with them, he will keep them at all costs," Gahn Irokai said.

Taliok made a choked sound.

"I agree with you." I paused, wondering how to broach the next part, then decided to just forge forward with it. "When you told me of Taliok's news, I was glad. I was hoping we could ally ourselves against Gahn Fallo."

Taliok started pacing again, his fists clenching and unclenching at his sides. Gahn Irokai watched him, then came to a quick decision.

"This is something that will affect all the people of the Sea Sands. This is the future of our tribes. We cannot have Gahn Fallo in control. We will stand with you against him. We will ride back tonight and gather our forces immediately. If we ride hard, night and day, we can make the journey home and back here in three days' time."

I grunted. This was acceptable.

Taliok raised his tail so quickly I barely registered the movement before stalking out of the tent, followed by Oxriel. Gahn Irokai raised his tail, as did I, before he left, too. I turned to Galok.

"Go with them. Help them ready their irkdu, and give them valok and meat."

Galok turned to follow my orders, letting the tent flap fall closed behind him as he left. I was relieved that Gahn Irokai had agreed to ally with us. But I was still wary. We hadn't talked about what would happen after we were victorious against Gahn Fallo. I could easily be trading one enemy for another.

But those thoughts would have to wait. Because now it was just my mate and me, alone in my tent. And every part of my body was painfully aware of her.

She was chattering away, gesturing wildly after the men who had left. She moved from my side, walking around the perimeter of the tent, examining the various things in my home. There wasn't much – my dakrival hide bed, my seat, some bone shelves with valok plants and candles, and extra weapons. I watched her as she moved from item to item, her eyes bright, her voice quick-spirited. There was an analytical intelligence about her. I got the sense she was trying to understand everything she saw.

"Zeezee," she said, hitting her chest. "Buroudei." She pointed at me. Then she pointed at the wall of the tent.

She was trying to learn more words. Pride swelled inside me. My mate certainly was intelligent. She wanted to understand this place, wanted to understand our language. Then I remembered that she already knew some words, like ablik and valok. Fierce jealousy pierced me as I thought of another Sea Sand man teaching her those things. Not for the first time, questions about who she was and where she'd come from burned inside me. But I had no way to ask.

She was still pointing at the tent, her slim finger poking at it as she watched me questioningly.

"Dakrival hide," I said. "Tent. *Tent.*"

She repeated the word, scrunching up her face as she garbled the pronunciation. I could not help but smile. It was adorable. I moved forward almost without noticing, like a drizelfly drawn to flame. She was pointing at other things now, and I indulged her demanding finger. It felt good to be able to give her something, to understand what she wanted.

"Bone shelf. Shelf. Axe. Valok candle. Sand."

She nodded, her face drawn in concentration as she took in each word, repeating it all dutifully. Then she started miming various actions. She brought her hand to her mouth as if eating.

"To eat."

She took that in, working her mouth around the sounds.

"To eat valok," she said, and I wanted to burst with admiration for her intelligence.

"Eat valok. You eat valok. I eat valok," I corrected her gently. She nodded, repeating my sentences. Then she started walking back and forth, before stopping and looking at me expectantly.

"To walk. You walk. Zeezee walks."

She nodded again, then started to run, her breasts bouncing beneath the woven peet grass tunic.

I cocked my head, as if in confusion. I knew what she wanted. But I wanted to see her body bounce more as she ran. She ran a little zigzag around the tent, and as she passed by me I caught her arm.

"To run."

Before she could repeat after me, I brought my mouth down to hers.

This time I opened my mouth to her right away. I did not hesitate. And neither did she.

CHAPTER THIRTEEN
Cece

OK, Buroudei was definitely getting the hang of the whole kissing thing. But then again, how could he not be good at it with three tongues? The centre part of his tongue lapped against mine, the outer ones swirling against my teeth and the insides of my cheeks. When his fangs grazed the inside of my lower lip I couldn't help but groan into his mouth, sensation rocketing down my body and between my legs. His skin was so warm under my hands. *Hold on.* When had my hands moved to his waist? Apparently my body was just doing whatever the hell it pleased now.

Maybe it's not just your body that's pleased.

My cheeks burned with the realization. There was no denying the raw, animal attraction that existed between us. And I couldn't even pretend it was just that. Outside, when everyone had been going crazy and drawing weapons left and right, I had been worried. Really, truly worried, that he would get hurt. I was starting to care about my alien gladiator. And caring for him seemed like a very bad idea.

But then again... was it that bad? It's not like I had a hope in hell surviving this planet without him. It made sense to try to form a connection with him. So far he'd proven himself to be protective of me and even sort of kind. So what if he was a bit scary, and apparently super horny? The wetness building between my legs told me that he wasn't the only one.

Maybe we're more alike than I thought.
But when he once again pulled aside his loincloth, the idea that we were alike shattered into a million tiny pieces. That was absolutely not a human cock.

For one thing, it was huge. And Buroudei's whole body, besides his head, was hairless. The copper sheen of his skin faded into rich brown and black at his groin, the same way it did at his forehead, feet, and the tip of his tail. There didn't seem to be any foreskin that I could see – the whole shaft and head was one smooth, dark organ. It thickened at the base, with two smaller spikes of flesh on either side, mimicking his three-part tongue. It was almost trident-like. Not going to lie, it was an extremely impressive setup. But not one that I was ready to have inside me just yet.

Um... Yet?

Buroudei was growling something against my neck, his hands squeezing my ass. The first time he'd done that, when we'd just met, it had seemed abominably rude. Now, apparently I couldn't get enough, and my hips arched against him hungrily. Before I could talk myself out of it, I let a finger slip down his hard chest and abdomen, gently touching his tip. God, the skin there was hot. And just as hard as the rest of him.

The glimmers of his eyes were spread wide across his eyes. His nostrils flared as I stroked his tip lightly.

He was staring at me silently, totally still, his hands frozen and tight against me. The fact I had brought this monster to a total standstill with just the touch of my hand was totally insane. And totally hot. I moved my hand faster, and watched in fascination as his lip drew back from his fangs.

I moved my hand down to explore the two smaller spikes of flesh on either side of his cock. For academic purposes, of course. They stood upright, alongside his cock, but they weren't nearly as hard. The flesh was pliable yet firm, almost like cartilage. I had both my hands down there now, each hand gently stroking and pressing on the small spikes. Buroudei groaned something unintelligible, and I watched his tip grow wet, the shaft twitching as his dark balls grew tight against his body. *Well, that's something like human men, at least.*

I thought about things I had done with human men, wondering how they'd translate. I wondered if I could make him come like this, just from touching. Heat pooled between my legs, and my breath came in ragged pants as I tightened my grip on his main shaft, beginning to pump my hand.

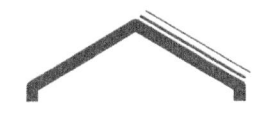

CHAPTER FOURTEEN
Buroudei

Curse me one hundred thousand times. I did not know what I had done to deserve it, but apparently my fate was to have a sadistic mate. Zeezee did not seem to want me to mate her, and instead tortured me like this, running her small, smooth hand against my hardness. It was a beautiful sort of torture, and I'd endure it forever, but it took everything I had not to throw her to the ground and rut her right there.

But no, I would control myself. My Zeezee was breakable and soft. And I would only do what she wanted, no matter how it pained me. Though it certainly pained me now. My whole body ached to claim her, my cock pulsing with need. And still she moved her hand maddeningly slowly, down to press on the cock spears, then back to the centre of my shaft. She gripped me harder, moving faster, and I clenched my fangs together, jaw clicking.

Everything about her was so soft. Her hand. Her skin. Her tongue. Would her cunt be that sweetly soft, too? The thought almost had me spilling seed right there, and my hand shot down, gripping her wrist. Then I grabbed her around her hips, hoisting her upward. I groaned in satisfaction as her legs automatically circled my waist and she clung to me. Her wetness soaked my abdomen and the base of my cock, and my head swam. I adjusted my hands, supporting her lush ass, and my cock settled along her crease, the head poking out where her tail would have normally been. But there was no tail, just the naked cheeks of her rump.

Zeezee was moaning and moving her hips of her own accord. It was glorious, seeing her lose herself in pleasure against my body, a vision of beauty like none I had ever seen before. *Soon I will drive her to this pleasure and beyond. When I'm inside her.* The spikes on either side of my cock were pressed upward under the weight of her body, their lengths slicking through her folds, their tips meeting against that nub of pleasure I had tasted earlier. Unable to hold back anymore, my hips began to grind back and forth, my cock growing slick with her wetness. Being so close to the entrance of her cunt, yet not inside, was tantalizing and agonizing.

I stared down at my mate, in total awe of her, holding her tighter as if to make sure she was not a mirage. A trick of the Sea Sands. But she was not. She was real and solid and bucking against me like a fiend, her mouth fallen open in pleasure. Her nipples had hardened beneath her tunic, and with a snarl, I readjusted my grip, freeing one hand to yank the clothing from her body. She did not fight me, but only nestled closer once the garment was gone, her hands holding fast to my shoulders as we moved against each other. Her breasts, soft and plump, pressed against me, her nipples like sweet little pebbles dragging over my skin as she arched. I could tell she was getting close to coming again – her muscles were clenching against the top of my shaft, her thighs tightening around me. I was getting close, too, my balls drawing tight, pleasure unfurling its coils inside me. It was considered bad luck to spill seed outside of a woman. But I could not help that at this point. Besides, what could such a thing do to me now? Was I not already the luckiest Gahn of the Sea Sands, to have found such a mate? Luck had no bearing here. Only fate. And fate had already found me.

"Buroudei... Buroudei," Zeezee could barely get my name out. It was slurred, then marred by cries that got louder and louder. Her legs were locked so tightly I wondered if I would ever escape. Not that I wanted to. *My Zeezee is stronger than I thought.*

I nuzzled downwards, my fangs dragging across her smooth cheek, forcing her head back. I claimed her mouth as she came, everything in her tightening and pulsing. Her hips jerked along my cock frantically, and I had to release her mouth to roar as I joined her, all my pent up desire spurting up along her back and onto the sand.

I held her, breathing hard against me, for a long time. I ignored the nagging feeling that this wasn't quite enough, that I needed to be inside her, needed to claim her. This would have to be enough for now. Every time she let me come that little bit closer was a gift to be cherished.

I carried her over to my hides, placing her down gently. She spoke to me, her words quick, her cheeks red, sitting up and glancing around, as if unsure what to do. Seeing her naked in my bed was going to be the death of me, but I steadied myself, laying down and dragging her against me. She squawked in protest, but stilled after a moment as I pulled her in, curling her back against my chest. I breathed deeply against her hair, savouring the moment, deeply content. Zeezee was muttering something, but her words were slowing, her breathing becoming regular. Her eyelids flickered closed, and then, she slept. I dragged a dakrival hide over her sleeping form and settled back in once again, burying my face in her hair.

And it was like that, breathing in her scent, revelling in the feeling of her skin against mine, that I finally slept.

《 》

I ROSE EARLY THE NEXT day, just as dawn was beginning to brush the edges of my tent. Zeezee was sound asleep, and I stared at her in the dim morning light, unable to fully believe that she was still here. That yesterday hadn't all been some torturous dream. But she was here – hair strewn about, limbs tossed widely, her mouth open as she made little snorting sounds in her sleep. *What a delightful woman.* My love for my mate was a glowing ember, warming my chest. I could have watched her sleep all day. But time did not allow for that. I had to speak to my men and start preparations for our battle with Gahn Fallo.

I dressed quickly, strapping my loincloth and weapons to my body. I was ready to leave the tent, but I realized I couldn't leave Zeezee there alone. She seemed to be getting closer to me, trusting me more, but I still didn't know that she wouldn't run the first chance she got. Frowning, I retied my long hair into its usual braid, then stepped outside my tent.

Galok was already up and strolling towards me. He raised his tail in greeting as he approached.

"Galok, will you get Rika and bring her here?"

Galok looked surprised, then concerned.

"You need the healer? It certainly sounded like everything was going well last night." His sight stars clouded, and his voice fell. "She is so small. Could she not take you? Did mating injure her?"

"No." My voice was flat. "I wish Rika to watch over her, and show her around while we are readying the men."

He looked relieved.

"I understand."

Galok bounded away. As I waited, I poked my head back in the tent. Zeezee had rolled over, gathering the dakrival hides tightly around herself like a drizelfly in its cocoon.

A moment later, Galok returned, followed by Rika.

"Galok and I have to ready the men for battle with Gahn Fallo. We mean to retrieve the other females, aided by Gahn Irokai. Keep Zeezee with you. She may travel anywhere within the tents of our people, but is never to be left alone."

"Yes, Gahn," Rika said, raising her tail, then heading inside my tent.

I turned to Galok. "Come. We must gather the men."

The message spread quickly through the ranks, and warriors began to gather at the central fire pit. Galok and I waited side by side for the rest of our ranks to arrive. Soon, all the men were gathered, and women and children watched from the outskirts. I took a deep breath, ready to speak.

It was time to tell them of Zeezee. To tell them of the new women. And to tell them what was to be done.

CHAPTER FIFTEEN
Cece

I woke up sweating. Though the tent provided protection from the sun, it was still hot as hell in there, especially in the blanket burrito I had created around myself. I disentangled myself from the heavy hides, pulling my sticky hair away from my face as I sat up. My muscles felt relaxed and languorous. *Yeah, two insane orgasms in a night will do that to a girl.*

Strangely, I didn't feel any shame about last night. It had felt weirdly... right. There was no denying Buroudei and I were getting closer. What exactly that meant, I couldn't be sure. But I wasn't exactly unhappy about it. I felt the shadow of a smile flicker across my lips as I turned to see where he was.

I gasped and reared back, yanking the blankets back up despite the heat. There was an alien here, but it wasn't Buroudei. I squinted, realization dawning.

"Rika?"

Rika's tail swished and she dipped her head in a way that I could only imagine was some kind of acknowledgement. I nodded slowly, reaching for the tunic that had dropped to the floor last night.

"Did you leave this for me at the other tent? Thank you."

I slipped it on over my head, catching a whiff of myself when my arms were up. *Yikes.*

"Doesn't look like you guys have much water around here, but is there anywhere to wash?"

I mimed smelling myself and making a face, then pretended to scrub under my arms.

Rika watched me with her head cocked and what I swore was the small pull of an amused smile. She was seated next to me on the sand, but she stood, then, clearly understanding what I was asking. I stood too, and as I did I felt the tension of a full bladder. *Oh God. How am I going to ask about that?*

"Um… Where…" I looked around, face on fire, trying to find a delicate way to ask about where I was supposed to pee. *Screw it.* Maybe there was no delicate way. I squatted on the ground in a pantomime of peeing, then jumped up, hoping she caught my drift. Her smile got bigger.

She grabbed a valok plant from among the items on the shelves in the tent, slicing one half of the round skin off. She gave me the open part to eat from, which I took. She kept her half of the hard rind in her hand, beckoning me to follow. I did so, slurping all the way.

The sun outside was beating down with ferocity, though it didn't seem very high in the sky yet. The sand was hot on my feet, and I half walked, half ran, bringing my knees up, trying to keep my feet in contact with the ground as little as possible. I finished the valok gel, then pulled my arms inside the short-sleeved tunic, trying to keep my head down and face out of the direct sun. I was 99% sure I'd gotten a wicked sunburn, along with all my other ailments, yesterday, that Rika had miraculously patched up. If I could avoid that this time around, that'd be swell. Rika watched me with interest, and I offered her a paltry smile.

"Yeah, I probably look crazy to you, eh?"

She answered me with a quick quip.

She took me just outside of the tents to an area of boulders. I made a beeline for a long shadow cast by the largest boulder, keeping my eye firmly on the dino-centipedes I saw grazing on the other side of the huge rocks. Rika didn't seem bothered by the huge animals, and she sidled up next to me. She held her valok rind up, indicating that I should do the same with the empty rind I now had. I snaked my arms out of the tunic and watched.

She used her valok rind to dig a small hole in the sand. She pretended to squat over it, then stood and filled the hole in with sand.

OK, seems easy enough.

I dug a small hole the way she had, then squatted. I began to relieve myself, sighing, only to realize that Rika was still staring.

"Jesus! Privacy not a big thing for you guys?"

She said something I did not understand, and I did my best to ignore her. It was pretty unlikely she'd ever seen anyone like me before. I couldn't blame her for being curious, especially if she was some kind of doctor. I quickly finished my business and filled the hole in, tossing the valok rind down to the sand. Rika tossed hers, as well. Then we began walking back to the tents, me with my arms tucked firmly back into the tunic, my hair doing a mostly crappy job of shielding my face. If I was going to survive any length of time in this place, I had to go back to the ship for supplies – extra clothing, sunscreen, and spare boots.

As we walked through the tents, I noticed that everything was pretty quiet. Nobody seemed to be around. *I wonder where everyone is.* I tried to ignore the fact that by "everyone" I really meant Buroudei. I couldn't stop wondering about him. There was an ache, deep in my abdomen, that had taken root. An ache I was pretty sure his absence caused.

I saw everyone else soon enough. A large group was gathered where the fire last night had been blazing. Approximately thirty men stood in a clump, and on the outskirts of the group was a much smaller collection of women and children. Something about the balance seemed off.

"Why are there so few women?" I blurted, suddenly realizing why the population seemed so skewed. Rika clearly didn't understand my question, and she gestured to a tent just ahead of us. We kept walking past the group, but I couldn't stop myself from staring. At the centre of everything, keeping everyone's attention rapt, was Buroudei. He was speaking, his deep voice booming with authority, his arms outstretched in some massive gesture. His skin gleamed beneath his blades in the sun, his muscles tightening and rippling with every movement. It seemed like he was these people's leader, and I'd heard more than one person refer to him as *Gahn*. I wondered if it meant something like "king." Or maybe, considering all the blades strapped to his body, "warlord." Despite the heat, a shiver ran through me to witness him – to see him commanding everyone with such power. Everyone, even the other strong-looking warriors, was standing still, deeply respectful and attentive as Buroudei spoke. My ears strained to understand him, even though I knew that would do no good. Alien language learning had been slow-going so far. Unfortunately. I chewed my lip as the group moved out of view. I really, really wanted to be able to talk to him. The intensity of that desire caught me off guard. This wasn't simple curiosity about a new language. This wasn't an academic thing. I wanted to talk *to him*. To learn about him, understand him, figure out what made him tick. Although, so far, it kind of seemed like what made him tick was me.

Rika pulled aside the flap of the tent we had reached. This one was different than the others. It was smaller, tall and narrow, with an opening at the top. She led me inside.

There wasn't much inside the tent. A small pit was in the centre, and along the perimeter of the tent were random-seeming objects like small rocks and collections of dried grass and some other plants I hadn't yet encountered. I stood, unsure of what we were doing here, when Rika bent and grabbed a couple of the small dark stones from the ground. She placed some of the dried grass in the pit, then smacked the stones together until a spark flew onto the dried grass, igniting immediately.

If I hadn't been sweating before, I sure was now. It was already hot in here, and the fire was adding to it. I coughed as smoke began to billow. It didn't smell like wood smoke – it was more herbal than that. Not altogether unpleasant, other than the fact that I was having trouble breathing. Eyes streaming, I felt Rika's hand on my shoulder. She pushed me down to the ground, below the smoke line, and my vision cleared as I sat. Before I knew what was happening, she had pulled her tunic up and over her head, sitting before me totally naked.

My cheeks grew doubly hot as I tried not to stare. A quick look told me that her body was strong and powerful, though her skin was starting to show signs of age. She also seemed to be, apart from some decent pectoral muscling, completely flat-chested. A glance between her legs (she was sitting cross-legged, so it was kind of hard to avoid) told me that she was indeed female, though. No hair anywhere on her body, besides her head. She pointed to my tunic, her claw catching on the fabric.

When in Rome...

I yanked it off, crossing my arms over my chest.

Rika grabbed at some of the plants that were on the ground. They looked like succulents, similar to the valok plants, but long and thin where the valok plants were flat and round. She used her claw to slice the end off of one of the long green spires, then squeezed some milky green gel out, the way you'd squeeze toothpaste from a tube. She handed the plant to me, and I watched as she began rubbing the gel into her skin. It didn't lather up, but it seemed to glide over her skin in such a way that it helped dissolve and remove dirt and oil. She reached over to what I had thought was more dried grass and picked up what was actually a rag of some kind, woven from plant matter. She swiped at her skin with the cloth, then waved the cloth in the air, drawing smoke towards her and over her skin. While it wasn't exactly the shower I had been craving, there was something kind of spa-like about it all.

I squeezed some of the cactus gel into my hands, running it over my body the way Rika had done. It had a somewhat sharp, but overall pleasant smell. It reminded me of something from back on earth. *Thyme.* The sudden connection to my home planet made my eyes prick with tears, and I distracted myself by scrubbing the gel into my skin. Rika handed me one of the woven rags, and I used that until, all in all, I felt pretty clean. The cactus gel stuff had basically evaporated off of my skin, leaving it smooth and soft. I was still sweating from the heat, but I didn't stink now. The only thing left was my hair, which I wasn't sure what to do with, but Rika saw to that, too.

She settled herself into a seated position behind me, and squeezed the last of the cactus stuff onto my scalp, working it through my hair. She moved gently, tackling my sweat-sticky tangles with her claws. Once again, like I had been when she had brought me food, I was reminded of Grammy, and the prickle of tears I had felt a moment ago became a full-on deluge. This simple act of kindness – the combing of my tangled hair – in a place as hostile as this planet had turned out to be, was breaking my heart. I pressed the palms of my hands against my eyes, sobbing as Rika muttered soft words to me. I was so grateful that Buroudei and his people had found me. I only wished the other women had had the chance for that same kindness.

Soon enough, Rika was finished. I sniffed, hard, swiping at the last of my tears as she pulled my hair into a clean, neat braid. Like it had from my skin, the gel had completely evaporated off of my hair, leaving it feeling smooth and smelling halfway-decent. She showed me how to use the empty cactus husk to clean my teeth and tongue. When we left the tent, I felt weak and wobbly and oddly renewed.

The sun was hotter now, and I shielded my face with my hand.

"Where's my jacket, and my pants? My boots?"

I pointed to the sun, then my skin, viciously shaking my head. Then I mimed pulling on a jacket and pointed to my legs and feet. I hated the idea of wearing those horrible bloodied pants, but there was no way I'd last out here much longer without my Canadian white-girl skin cooking in the sun. Rika seemed to understand my meaning, and led me quickly to the largest tent, which wasn't far from the sauna tent. I ran inside, trying to get out of the sun, and almost smacked into another alien.

"Oh! Sorry," I said, stopping short. I looked up at who I'd almost toppled.

Well, not like I'd be able to topple one of these guys. But still.

This alien wore a similar tunic to Rika and me. Large eyes and a soft mouth gave her face a pretty, in an alien sort of way, look. Definitely another female, though younger than Rika. Her hair was shining and black, her skin richly coloured and smooth. I smiled, and she gave me a small smile back. I squealed, then, when something latched onto my waist. The new alien made a distinctly maternal tsking sound, and yanked a small alien – a girl, I thought – from my torso.

I had no idea to gauge how old the child was. She was grinning, the shimmers of her eyes pulsing mischievously. Based on her behaviour and the youthfulness of her face, I would have guessed she was maybe the equivalent to an Earth six-year-old. But much, much bigger.

The adult alien said something to me quickly, and I had a feeling she was apologizing for the child. I noticed a similarity in the soft mouths smiling at me. *It's her daughter.*

I smiled widely.

"Don't worry about it! I'm Cece."

The other woman looked confused, her eyes darting to Rika. Rika spoke quickly, gesturing towards me. I didn't catch much of what she said besides, "Zeezee." Then Rika gestured to the other two, looking at me. "Balia," she said, pointing to the adult. "Zofra" was the child. I grinned.

"Nice to meet you, Balia and Zofra."

They both smiled, then raised their tails in front of their eyes. *I wonder what that means.* I'd seen that gesture several times now. Maybe some kind of greeting.

"Sorry I don't have a tail, or I'd do the same right back at you."

Balia smiled vaguely at my unfamiliar words, but Zofra started chattering to me animatedly, not caring that I had no idea what she was saying. I nodded, grinning at her, trying to take in whatever she was saying. She took me by the hand and led me around the tent, showing me various items. I did my best to keep track of her rapid-fire dialogue, logging away whatever words I could catch onto for later analysis. I was pretty sure I'd learned at least a few more words, like the words for jar, bandage, and bed. As Zofra gave me the tour, Rika and Balia talked in hushed tones. A few moments later, Rika approached with a small bundle. My clothes.

After my sauna scrub, the filthy clothes seemed especially unappealing.

"Thanks," I said with a half-hearted smile. I yanked my stiff, stained pants on, wincing at the feeling of the crunchy dried blood against my skin. Then went on the socks and the boots, followed by my solar protection jacket. I didn't bother with my dirty tank top and underwear, instead balling them up and placing them down discreetly in a corner. Zofra bounded over to my discarded garments, looking like she was about to pick them up and examine them closely, but her mother swatted her away.

"Yeah, you should probably burn those." I laughed awkwardly, but it wasn't really a joke.

Once I was dressed, I felt a little more prepared to head back outside. Rika spent the rest of the day with me, showing me around and helping me get accustomed to how things worked in their tiny tent village. I didn't get to talk to many of the men – after the morning meeting they all dispersed to their various tasks, many of them leaving for what looked like hunting or guard duties, others sharpening weapons. I did get to meet the women, of which there were only ten, plus their children. The women welcomed me with a shy sort of friendliness. One woman, whom Rika called Zanixia, seemed a little more reserved than the others, but in general they all seemed glad to meet me. The children were especially excited, many of them coming up to me and touching my skin and hair and nose while babbling enthusiastically.

As Rika led me around throughout the day, I found my eyes searching for Buroudei. I wondered what he was doing, where he was, and who he was talking to. As lovely as Rika had been, I kind of wished he was the one showing me around. OK, there was no "kind of" about it. I wished I was with him.

It may not have been rational or reasonable or sane. But I missed him. I missed him way, way more than I should have.

And it kind of scared the shit out of me.

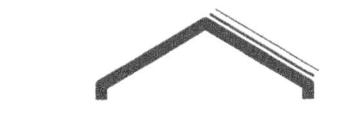

CHAPTER SIXTEEN
Buroudei

"She is very fragile. Very fragile."

Rika's voice was stern. We were standing outside of my tent. Zeezee was inside, and all I wanted to do was see her after not being near her for the entire day. Being apart from her was causing me physical pain.

"I know, Rika," I said impatiently. "But I will protect her."

Rika frowned, her tail thrashing.

"No, Gahn, you do not understand. She was not created for a place like this. Did you know even the sun hurts her skin? It burns her like fire. That is why she must wear her strange clothing."

My heart sank. This was worse than I had thought. I had hoped that, after being healed by Rika, Zeezee would somehow permanently be alright. But that was clearly not the case. How was it possible that even the sun was harmful to her? A terrible helplessness clawed at me.

"I will not pretend to be wiser than you, Rika. Tell me what to do."

I did not like the desperation in my voice. It made me feel weak. Zeezee was a vulnerability like no other. But I meant what I'd said. Whatever needed to be done, I would do it. I could not accept that my mate was not meant for my world. She would be strong. She would survive. I would make it so. Whether through blood or sweat or sheer force of will, I would make it so.

"I wish I knew what to tell you, my Gahn." There was a pained sincerity to Rika's voice. "Without being able to speak to her, it is hard to know what she needs." She paused then, her eyes losing focus, staring out over the sands beyond the boulders. "I did notice that many times throughout the day she looked out across the sand. Towards the place you found her. Maybe she left something behind. Something she needs."

I clenched my jaw. I had no interest in bringing Zeezee back over the open sands to the scene of the zeelk slaughter.

"It is too dangerous for her. You know that."

Rika levelled her gaze at me.

"You may not have another choice."

She said no more, leaving me to brood over her words under the star-pricked sky. I mulled over my options. I could go without her and scope out the site on my own. But then again, I wouldn't even know what I was looking for there. Zeezee was the only one who knew what she needed. And she could not tell me. I sighed roughly, staring up at the sky. The zeelk were likely lured by the sound of the big flying creature landing. It would have sent vibrations down into the sand, calling them up. If we went quietly, just the two of us, it may not be too dangerous. *And like Rika said, I may not have another choice.* I did not like this. Not having choices. Not knowing which path to take. Grimly, I entered the tent.

Much of the tension I felt evaporated when I saw my mate's small, lovely face. She had been seated on my hides, and she scrambled to her feet, speaking animatedly. Then, almost shyly, slowly, as if trying to get it just right, she said our word for "hello."

My tail thumped the sand, warmth filling my chest. She must have learned that today with Rika. What a glorious thing, to have your mate waiting for you at your tent, ready to greet you like that. Such happiness was almost beyond comprehension. I went to her at once, cupping her jaw in my hands, before lowering my mouth to hers. Her lips parted quickly, welcoming me. But it didn't last long. She pulled back quickly, saying something rapid in her language before switching to the tongue of the Sea Sands.

"Buroudei to eat meat."

Her brow crumpled inward, as if she knew that wasn't quite right (it wasn't) but I was honoured by her effort all the same. She shook her head quickly, then grabbed a bone plate from the nearby shelf.

On the plate was a choice selection of dakrival meat from tonight's feast. I hadn't joined the tribe for the meal – I had been too busy with Galok, planning our raid on Gahn Fallo. I took the plate from her small hand, sitting down, curling my tail around myself, patting the dakrival hide next to me. Her cheeks red, she sat, smoothing the tunic over her knees as she drew them up to her chest. Seeing her in the clothing of our people, with her hair braided like ours, was going right to my groin. I grunted, turning my attention to my meal, eating quickly. Soon, I would have a much sweeter taste upon my tongues.

I finished the food, tossing the plate aside, then leaned over. Zeezee's eyes got wide as I settled one hand behind her back on the sand, the other hitching at the hem of her tunic, yanking it up over her hips, revealing her soft thighs and that dark patch of hair that was so very odd and so very enticing. Need was coursing through me, hot and hard. I had been away from her too long today. *Tonight I will mate her.*

But, as I should have come to expect by now, my lovely little mate had other plans. Just as I was lowering my head to lap at the goodness between her legs, I felt something small but strong close around one of my ears, halting my head's descent. I stopped, letting my eyes roll upward to look at Zeezee's face. One of her hands was clenched around one of my ears, her other hand was wagging her finger in my face in a gesture I did not recognize. I bit back a growl of irritation. Though I did not recognize the gesture, I could understand the meaning. *Stop what you are doing this instant.*

This woman, my mate, the strange and perfect creature who had brought such renewed meaning to my life, would most certainly be the death of me.

CHAPTER SEVENTEEN
Cece

It was getting easier and easier to be swept up in Buroudei's alien seduction techniques. Not that he exactly had seduction techniques beyond *you're here, I'm here, let's do stuff*. But more and more, I wasn't questioning whatever it was that was between us. After spending the day with Rika, I had been looking forward to seeing him, and when he'd walked into the tent I couldn't deny that my body had responded immediately – my heart rate increasing, my blood rushing hot, pulsing between my legs. The way he'd kissed me, so immediately, so naturally, had made me just a little too happy. It felt like I was meant to be here, like I belonged, like I had someone. And after losing Grammy and having no one, that was the most seductive thing of all.

So I really had to fight the urge to let my legs fall open under Buroudei's mouth. But I did so, the quickest way I could see: by grabbing one of his ears.

That did the trick. The look he gave me was a combination of *are you serious* and *I should have known*, but I hardened myself, wagging my finger, scooting my bottom back and away from him. We had to discuss serious things. I released Buroudei's ear, keeping a close eye on him, but he seemed to sense what I wanted, as unhappy as it appeared to make him. He raised his head back up, but did not adjust his position. He loomed over me, his hands on the sand on either side of my hips. His dark eyes swirled with copper stars, just inches from my own. I blinked, shifting my gaze to keep myself from falling headfirst into them. But then my gaze ended up on his mouth, and that was just as distracting. I settled firmly on his chin, face on fire, casting my mind back to the various words I had learned to try to craft my request.

"Buroudei Cece to walk sand."

Crap. That wasn't right. Not even close. I raised my gaze, unable to help myself, watching as the shimmering parts of Buroudei's eyes tightened up as he focused on me.

"Buroudei Cece to walk to retrieve sand."

Oh, God. I really needed to work on my verb conjugation. And I wasn't sure about the placement of the objects, direct or indirect. I was trying to tell him that I needed him to take me back out over the sand to the ship so that I could get some supplies. As terrible as it was, it seemed less and less likely every hour that any of my friends were left alive. But I was. I had survived. And I needed to do everything I could to ensure that survival. Buddying up with Buroudei and his people had been a big step towards that, but I needed more – more clothing and extra boots, more sunscreen, and whatever other useful stuff I could pull out of the cargo bay. Even the small amount of time I'd spent without my solar jacket today had left me sunburned, and Rika had had to smear some more of that radioactive milk on me to get things back to normal.

Buroudei hadn't moved. I could feel the puffs of his breath against my mouth, and my lips parted involuntarily. *Focus, Cece.* I had to make him understand my request. I knew he wouldn't let me just walk off alone, and I definitely wouldn't survive such a field trip alone.

"Buroudei Cece to walk... sand... to retrieve..." I blew out a frustrated breath. Now I was just rearranging the words I'd already said. My vocabulary was failing me. Half the stuff I needed to say they probably didn't even have a word for. I had a feeling that "space ship" wasn't something that would translate.

"Come on, I'll show you," I said in English, scooting back further and standing. Buroudei's tail twitched, and for a second it seemed like he was about to grab my ankle and yank me back down.

"Don't worry, I'm not going anywhere without you." I held out my hand.

He stared at it, then looked up at me questioningly.

"Come on, stand up!" I waved my arms up and down, bending and straightening my legs dramatically so that he'd get the picture. He did, getting to his feet, raising himself to his full, impressive height. I ignored the drying of my throat, the quickening of my pulse, and reached for his hand, taking it in my own. "This is what I was trying to get you to do. Holding hands." I gave his huge hand a squeeze, and watched in fascination as the specks of his eyes flew outward, his nostrils flaring.

"Not sure I like the look in your eye. Don't distract me. Let's go." I tugged on his hand, leading him out of the tent.

Outside, the night was cool. I pulled Buroudei around the side of the tent, thoroughly enjoying the way he was following without question. I stopped, pointing out over the desert, hopefully somewhat in the direction of the ship. It was way too far away to be visible from here.

"Buroudei Cece to walk to retrieve." With my free hand, I gestured violently out towards the horizon. Then I turned to look up at him. "Please, please understand me."

Buroudei said nothing, his face impossible to read. We faced each other in the gloom, and he captured my other hand with his, holding them between us. Then he uttered a sentence, some of which I actually understood... "*Something something* go *something something* retrieve..."

I gasped.

"Are you saying you know what I'm asking. You'll take me? You'll take me back to the ship?" I pointed out towards the horizon again, and Buroudei's tail twitched in acknowledgement. He repeated his sentence, and I was even more sure that time that he was agreeing to do what I'd asked.

I gave a whoop, almost as excited about our communication success as I was about actually going back to the ship, and I leaped forward, throwing my arms around his waist. I felt his tail thump the ground, hard, and his own arms wrapped around me, cradling me in a cage of steel. I pressed my forehead into his chest and sighed.

"Thank you."

Buroudei gave a low growl, then before I knew it he'd yanked me up, carrying me close against his chest, back into his tent. I thought about protesting, and kicking and fighting to be let down, but slowly I realized that I just didn't want to. I was flying high from the fact that we'd just talked to each other. Well, sort of. I was so excited by our new connection, and about the fact that he was going to help me. Tears burned in my eyes. It finally felt like I was making some kind of progress, that things were maybe starting to go alright after disaster after disaster. I looked up, almost dreamily, at Buroudei's strong jaw, his fierce expression, as he carried me into the tent.

"What's the next step up from 'I'm so happy I could kiss you'? I'm so happy I could fuck you?" God, I felt crazy, and maybe this was crazy, but I knew in that moment that if Buroudei tried something again, I would go for it.

But he didn't try anything. A soft "oof" of disappointment came out of my mouth involuntarily as Buroudei deposited me onto the collection of hides that was his bed. Then he stood, speaking softly, the only words I recognized being "dakrival hide" and "irkdu." I frowned, gesturing at the straining behind his loincloth.

"You should really stay and take advantage of this, buddy. I don't know if I'm going to feel this insane tomorrow."

Buroudei looked pained, but he spoke again, more quickly this time, his words coming like gruff barks. He bent and brushed his fingertips over my forehead, down my jaw, then down the length of my braid, fingering the smooth tail of my hair. I moved up to my knees, clutching at his hand, pressing it against my neck.

The sound he made was strangled as he pulled away. Without another word, he turned, leaving the tent, the flap falling closed behind him with a finality that made me want to cry.

"Well, fine then. Whatever. Go do whatever alien business is so pressing," I huffed. With an annoyed groan, I flopped down into the bed, pulling the hides around myself, burrowing down and nursing my pride. If Buroudei came back that night, I wasn't aware of it. I fell asleep alone, and did not dream.

⟨ ⟩

WHEN I WOKE THE NEXT morning, Rika was waiting for me once again. Similarly to yesterday, she remained glued to my side, and honestly, I was glad for the company. Though we couldn't understand each other's words, we were getting used to our unique language of gestures. I liked being around her, and that went for the other members of the tribe I'd gotten the chance to interact with, too. I kept my eyes peeled for Buroudei, unable to help myself. I caught flashes of him now and then, usually deep in conversation with an exceptionally tall warrior (exceptionally tall even by their standards), but like yesterday, he seemed extremely busy. I ignored the little niggle of pain I felt at not being able to spend time with him. *Stupid. You should be focusing on more important things.* More important things like when we'd be going back to the ship. I realized that Buroudei and I didn't have a way to communicate when that was happening. He'd said he'd take me, but when? He might not have understood how much I needed to go get my human supplies.

He didn't join us for the evening meal, and once again I ended up at his tent alone with a plate of food. *Why do I feel like I got stood up?* My feelings were ridiculous, but they were hurt all the same. When he finally did arrive, long after dark had fallen, I greeted him with a cold shrug, pointing to the plate. He looked at it, then slashed his tail, holding his hand out to me the way I had to him last night.

"Oh, so you don't even have time to eat the meal I slaved over?"

That was mostly a joke, of course. I had no idea what I was doing by the massive communal fire, and I just collected the pieces of meat that Rika had set aside for Buroudei. *This must be what women feel like when their husbands get home late for dinner.* I flushed. *Hold on, husband?* I hadn't been here that long, had I? Long enough that I was actually thinking about settling down with an alien?

We'll think about that one later.

Either way, I still took his hand.

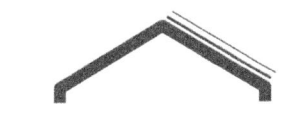

CHAPTER EIGHTEEN
Buroudei

I was a Gahn, certainly. But by now I should have been regarded as a true god among men for the restraint that I had shown. Zeezee had seemed different last night, like she would have actually welcomed my cock if I had offered it. Perhaps I was a fool for refusing.

A fool. A god.

Maybe both.

But there had been no time. Knowing that I had to prepare for our trip back to the fallen creature on top of the looming battle with Gahn Fallo meant that I had to use every spare moment I had. And that had meant leaving her in the tent so I could create her irkdu saddle and her riding garments. I could have assigned the task to one of the women, but it had felt important that I did it myself. The fact she'd gotten so injured the first time she'd ridden my mount with me was still a hot blade of shame in my guts. This was the smallest sort of recompense. I would learn every intricacy of her kind. I would learn exactly how to provide for her. I would spend the rest of my life making sure something like that never happened again.

And so I'd stayed up half the night, working the hides the way my mother had done when she was still alive. And after I'd finished, though I'd longed to plunge myself into Zeezee's warm, soft body, I'd slept at Galok's tent. She'd need her rest, too, for the journey.

Now that darkness had fallen, it was time. The zeelk were less active at night, and Zeezee wouldn't be as susceptible to the sun and heat. We didn't have many nights left before Gahn Irokai returned with his men. It had to be now.

Zeezee's hand was so small in mine. It made my heart ache. The full weight of her vulnerability was crashing down upon me. Just existing in my world was a danger to her. And now she was going to be in even more danger as we travelled back to the body of the fallen creature. I did not like it. Not at all. But I knew with increasing certainty that it had to be done. *Best to get it over with quickly.*

Zeezee said nothing as we walked, which was unusual for her. I'd been half-expecting her to try out any newly acquired words on me, and felt a pang in my chest when she didn't. *Perhaps her mind is on the journey ahead.*

I led Zeezee away from the tents, towards the boulders and the peet grass. The irkdu roamed slowly, munching on grass. Some of them slept. I whistled, sharp and low, and my mount roused itself, moving towards us.

Zeezee said something, then, and she sounded unhappy. I squeezed her hand, the way she'd squeezed mine yesterday.

"Do not worry, Zeezee. I have made better preparations this time."

I moved to where I'd stored our supplies between two of the smaller boulders. Zeezee clutched at my hand, following closely, keeping her eye warily pinned to my irkdu. It was wise of her – though my animal was well-trained and would not intentionally hurt her, it could crush her with one wrong roll of its huge body.

I had already collected everything I imagined we would need. We would likely be back before sunrise, but I had brought Zeezee's shielding cloak all the same, as well as the hard shells she wore on her feet during the day. The fabric garments she wore between her feet and the shells were wearing thin in places, so I'd fashioned her new ones from the softest, thinnest parts of the dakrival hide. I'd reinforced her leg garments with much tougher dakrival leather along the inner thighs, cutting away the bloodied parts, and had crafted a saddle of sorts using a frame of bone and more heaped layers of leather. We used saddles like these for our cubs when learning how to ride, when their legs were too short to comfortably remain seated, so I already knew the basic design. It was adorable, and terrifying, that I only had to make the saddle slightly larger for Zeezee than we would make them for our tribe's children. I had valok and dried meat to sustain us, tucked into the pockets of the saddle, as well as long leather cords to lash any other items to the irkdu. I had no idea what we were going back to collect, but we should have had enough to be prepared. Even if we were getting something large, it could trail behind the irkdu, tied with the cords. I had collected weapons, too: an extra zeelk spur spear, several knives, and my axe.

I presented Zeezee with her clothing, then got to work securing the saddle to the irkdu. Because I was turned away from her, working with the saddle, I did not see Zeezee's reaction to our supplies, and thus was blindsided when I turned around and found her eyes shining, her cheeks wet, her voice coming in short little wails. Rika told me Zeezee had done this in the smoke tent. Rika was fairly sure it was nothing physiological, not a sign of illness, but rather something to do with strong emotion. I abandoned the saddle and was at her side immediately, brushing my fingers across her wet cheeks.

"What is it? What is happening?"

What is happening? A question for the ages. A question I was asking myself far too often lately.

Zeezee was waving the thin leather foot coverings I'd made in the air between us, her words coming thick and fast. The wetness coming from her eyes was unnerving. Losing that amount of moisture in the desert, apart from normal daily bodily functions, was never a good sign. I pressed my fingers to her cheeks, applying a small amount of pressure upwards, as if I could somehow stem the flow. But that only seemed to make things worse.

"Save your fluids, mate, or I will need to collect more valok for our journey." I wished I knew what she was saying. She was very clearly talking about the foot coverings, and her tone was upset. I frowned, trying to look at the garments as she waved them frantically. I'd copied the design of the ones she'd come with, and the ones I made seemed far better constructed, the fabric softer and also more durable. But clearly I had done something wrong.

"I can adjust them. Give them here."

I tried to take them from her hands, but she yelped, hugging them to her chest with the ferocity of a krixel defending its kill, before bending and putting them on her feet. I watched her in confusion, and worried that, even if we one day shared the same language, I would never really understand her.

After putting on the foot coverings (that I saw with satisfaction seemed to fit well, despite whatever her protestations may have been) she pulled on her leg coverings. When she noticed my amendments to that garment, her eye leaking was renewed once more. I was at a loss. She didn't seem to want me to do anything, and I did not like that feeling. She wiped viciously at her cheeks then put on her hard foot shells.

She stood and faced me, and started trying to form a sentence. A question.

"Dakrival hide... Balia?"

I stared at her, confused. She sniffed hard, then tried again, this time pointing to the new parts of her pants, then her feet.

"Dakrival hide Balia? Rika?" She made a motion with her hands that looked like the sewing of hides. Was she asking who had made her garments? I couldn't see why that mattered.

"I made them last night." I gestured to myself. She didn't seem convinced that I understood her meaning, so I copied her sewing gesture then pointed to myself.

Absurdly, this made her face crumple inward in despair and her hands flew up, pressing hard against her eyes as her shoulders shook. Rika must have been wrong. Panic filled me. *Surely this is not normal.* I was about to reach for her when she tipped forward, pressing her hands and face into my chest. I grappled at her back, drawing her hard against me, as if by doing so I could undo whatever malady plagued her. And it worked, somewhat. Soon, her shuddering subsided, and she turned her damp face up to mine, saying one of her words that I did not recognize. Then she rose up on her little toes, pulling at my shoulders. She said something in irritation, then pointed at her mouth.

Now what? Something was wrong with her mouth?

She spoke more, then reached up to tap my mouth, then hers again. Her face was drawn tight with determination. She wanted something. Realization dawned, and with a groan, I lowered my mouth to hers. As her wet mouth opened under mine, I tried to remind myself of my ablik will. *I am a mighty Gahn. I will be a god among men. I will show such restraint that stories will be told of it round fires forever...*

My body did not care about such noble musings. My cock hardened, pressing hungrily against Zeezee's abdomen. She did not shy away, and her small hands moved back down to lock around my waist as she arched against me. I could not shake the image of replenishing the fluids she'd lost from her eyes with my own. I'd fill her until her cunt was dripping. *Or her mouth.* I hissed as my cock throbbed painfully in response to that image.

How men with mates got anything done was beyond me.

But, like it or not, we did have things to do. Though it pained me, badly, I pulled back from Zeezee, brushing away the last remaining wetness from her cheeks.

"We must go now." I smiled to myself, then imitated her garbled wording. "Buroudei Cece to walk to retrieve sand."

Zeezee licked her lips, her breathing ragged, but she smiled and nodded her head in a way I now recognized as "yes," her braid bouncing against her shoulder. Without further delay, I helped her up into the saddle.

CHAPTER NINETEEN
Cece

I sat stock still in the saddle, trying very hard to keep my shit together. We didn't need more tears now, but it was tough. Those socks were just so soft and small. The fact that somebody in the tribe cared enough about the lost human girl who barely spoke their language to make her new clothes and socks was already enough to set me off. And finding out it was actually Buroudei? Yeah, that was a whole other level. The image of him, bent over and sewing a garment as ridiculously small as one of these socks, making sure it would fit my puny human foot, was a shot straight to my goddamn heart.

I watched him as he frowned and muttered to himself, fussing with the saddle, tightening some things and adjusting others. I watched his muscles bunch, his jaw growing hard in concentration, his starkly beautiful eyes focused. Frankly, I was kind of wondering if he was even real. A strong warrior who seemed addicted to giving me pleasure, who'd made me a pair of freaking socks, plus new pants and a saddle? My last boyfriend couldn't have even been bothered to take the trash out.

Why was I comparing him to my last boyfriend?
What exactly is he to me?
My captor? My saviour? My big alien boyfriend?
Honestly, I had no idea. All I knew was that the closer we got, the less I wanted to be away from him.

Soon enough, Buroudei grunted in satisfaction at his handiwork, and I wiggled my hips, settling in. This was about a thousand times more comfortable than the last time I'd ridden on this thing. My legs felt supported and cushioned, and when Buroudei swung up behind me after securing all our supplies, I was able to lean back comfortably against him for support. My cheeks grew warm as he murmured something into my hair, his massive arm circling around me. His other hand gripped a spear, and I couldn't deny the brutal, purely masculine eroticism of that image. The warmth in my cheeks travelled down my neck, then lower and lower.

Buroudei barked at the irkdu, and then we were off.

The journey took hours. At least, I assume it took hours. I had no way to properly tell. I was amazed Buroudei could keep track of where we were going. So much of the way was rolling, featureless sand. Buroudei kept his eyes trained ahead of us, his weapon always at the ready, but nothing seemed to stir in the sand around us.

Eventually a set of cliffs appeared to our right, and I yelped, recognizing them. Buroudei grunted in acknowledgement. Those were the cliffs where he'd first taken me. That meant we were getting close.

The happiness and excitement I'd felt at getting successfully back to the ship transformed into a sick bundle of nerves. My stomach twisted, and I ground my teeth in anticipation of what I'd find. I was not looking forward to seeing the bodies of my friends, especially if I couldn't do anything for them. I had a feeling Buroudei wouldn't stand around guarding me while I tried to bury a bunch of half-eaten humans.

A dark form was taking shape on the horizon. I sat up straighter, pointing and exclaiming, "There it is! We're almost there."

Buroudei did not respond, but urged his irkdu forward with a click of his tongue. We crossed the last stretch of sand in what felt like no time at all. I held my breath as we approached.

The carnage of the scene was still laid bare. Though, shockingly, I didn't see the corpses of any of my friends. Instead, the sand was littered with the motionless bodies of the horrible crab monsters. Just seeing them, even lifeless, with their legs curled inward on themselves, was enough to make my skin crawl. Buroudei was sniffing the air, his head swinging back and forth as he surveyed the scene, spear half-raised. I didn't speak, too afraid to make a sound. But after a moment, he seemed to relax, though only slightly, and we continued forward.

When we passed by one of the dead alien monsters, Buroudei leaned down and yanked a spear from its body, growling something to himself and securing it to his mount.

"I don't see any of their bodies," I whispered, more to myself than Buroudei. I wasn't sure if that was giving me hope, or hinting at something even worse. Was it a good or bad sign that none of my friends were rotting out here? I had a good view into the bridge, and I saw the aftermath of the pilots and soldiers who had died there – scattered bones stripped clean of flesh, scraps of uniforms littering the floor. But that seemed to be limited to the initial attack area. I didn't see any more human gore out here, and something had obviously killed all the crab monsters. A flicker of painful hope came to life inside me.

Maybe they're all still alive out there.

I hadn't been told anything about how many aliens like Buroudei there were on this planet. I had no idea if there were other groups out there, or even other kinds of aliens, that could have rescued my friends. But for now, I was choosing to believe that they were still around. Somewhere. Someway.

I grinned, feeling a renewed sense of purpose. Things were already going well. We'd made it back to the ship without issue, and there was evidence that my friends were still alive? It was almost too good to be true. The thought that there were other humans on this planet, the women I'd spent two weeks working and living with, brought me intense joy. *Now I just have to figure out how to ask Buroudei to help me find them.*

I surveyed the ship, remembering why we'd come.

One thing at a time.

With Buroudei's help, I dismounted. If he hadn't been there, holding me every step of the way, I would have flopped to the sand in a tangle of discombobulated limbs. It was kind of awe-inspiring how graceful and strong he was.

"Thanks," I said, smiling up at him. He did not return my happy look. It was clear he wasn't glad to be here. I had to make this quick.

The only problem was I didn't really know where to start. I knew I wanted to avoid the mess in the bridge, so I circled around the back of the ship to the open cargo bay, followed closely by Buroudei, who now held a spear in one hand and his axe in the other. Just as I remembered from the brief time I'd been in this part of the ship, there were boxes and shelves lining the walls. Some things had been damaged, but a remarkable amount of stuff seemed untouched. I picked a random part of the room and started looking around, opening whatever boxes I could. A lot of the stuff was interesting, and potentially useful to someone, but not to me. Things like microscopes and lab equipment were passed over, but when I found a crate of water bottles, I literally jumped for joy. Dozens of plastic water bottles, shining like precious jewels, in neat little rows. I grabbed the first one in reach, cranking it open and chugging. The valok plants were OK, and they kept me hydrated enough, but there was nothing like pure water when you were thirsty.

Buroudei was watching me with concern.

"It's water! My home planet is covered in this stuff."

I poured a little in a stream onto the floor of the cargo bay, and Buroudei jerked back, then leaned forward with interest.

"Here, drink some!" I showed him how to drink from the bottle, and he did so, rather suspiciously. After a sip he handed it back, making a sour face that made me chuckle.

"You're so broody. Come on, help me get these out there, would you?" I gestured to the large crate, which weighed easily 80lbs, batting my eyelashes, only half-jokingly. Buroudei crouched then lifted the crate onto his shoulder, steadying it and holding it with only one arm so that he could keep his spear ready with the other. *Holy shit*. I tried not to gulp at the sheer, raw power of his body. To say it was impressive was an understatement.

We moved back outside, and Buroudei lashed the crate securely to the irkdu, just in front of the saddle. We made several trips in and out of the cargo bay. I was able to track down some extra clothing and two extra jackets. None of it was my size, but baggy was better than nothing. I also found an abandoned pack that still had all of the supplies for our original mission – the first aid stuff, the sunglasses, the rations and the sunscreen. We tied it all to the irkdu, the giant animal starting to look more and more like some kind of mutant pack mule. As Buroudei tightened the straps against the backpack, I stared at the broken front part of the ship, smashed to bits by the alien crabs.

No chance that thing will fly again.

A jolt went through me. How was it that this was the first time that the thought of returning to Earth had even crossed my mind? We'd come all the way back to this ship, a *space ship*, for God's sake, and I hadn't once wondered if we could somehow get it up and running, or at least make some sort of transmission for our rescue? I'd only wanted to come back here for supplies, nothing more. What the hell did that say about me? Did I not want to go back?

My gaze drifted to Buroudei. Involuntarily. Inevitably. Like his body was emitting some kind of gravity. He'd been protective and good, in his alien way. He'd looked out for me, tried to take care of me, and made me feel, every moment, like I was his, even if that was sometimes extremely annoying. What did I have back on Earth? No one. Nothing. A government that had betrayed me and sent my friends and me to almost certain death. I had my PhD program, I guessed, but what was more fulfilling to a linguist than studying an alien language, up close and personal? The realization crystallized inside me so hard and fast it cracked, radiating pain through my rib cage. I had nothing on Earth. Nothing worth going back for. But here? Maybe here I had something. Or someone.

I have to tell him.

In this short time, as crazy as it seemed, I'd grown to care for my tall, brooding, alien gladiator. I had to let him know, somehow. My chest was tight with the need to let out this mounting emotion. I moved towards him, placing my hands on his chest, tilting my chin upward. My voice was choked as I spoke his name.

"Buroudei..."

A ferocious roar split the air. The breath whooshed painfully out of me as Buroudei slammed me to the ground, covering me with the bulk of his body as a spear soared over us.

What the hell?

If we were going to run into trouble out here, I thought it would have been more of the crab things. Not one of Buroudei's men.

In a crouch, Buroudei dragged me over to the irkdu, settling me against its body before whirling, spear and axe drawn. His tail thrashed back and forth in the sand and his breath came in a feral hiss. I panted, trying to regain my breath and some semblance of understanding of the situation. But my brain was clearly two steps behind Buroudei's. I hadn't even focused my eyes when he'd located the threat and had gone stalking out over the sands toward it. He was growling and roaring, bitter, sharp words I didn't understand. The irkdu snuffled, and I stood, staying somewhat bent, clutching at the animal's side as I tried to gauge just what the fuck was happening.

Buroudei jerked, and a knife thudded to the ground behind him. I cried out without meaning to. The darkness was lit by this planet's spinning belt of asteroids, glowing like moons, and I could see the blade had grazed his shoulder. Black blood streamed down his arm, but Buroudei didn't seem to notice. His entire focus was on the man approaching us from the ship.

I said man, but it was another alien. The same kind of alien as Buroudei, but I realized that I didn't recognize him at all from Buroudei's tribe. This was a stranger. A threat. My pulse thundered. *If Buroudei gets hurt because of this, because of me...* The thought was too painful to bring to completion.

They moved so quickly I could barely register what had happened. One moment they were moving towards each other, weapons drawn, the next they were locked in brutal battle, limbs and tails flying, blades flashing. I froze in horror, watching them. This wasn't some schoolyard scuffle. It was plain as day that this was a fight to the death. My fear was explosive and overpowering, and I screamed Buroudei's name.

And he looked. Of course he looked. Because he always looked at me, for me, after me. Because, for some reason, I was dear to him. Beyond measure. Beyond words. So when I called for him, he looked. He looked at me like I was the only thing in the world.

But clearly he was looking at a complete fucking idiot, because that one single stupid scream of his name changed the tide of the battle. Changed the tide of everything.

Because of the distraction, the other alien got the upper hand, managing to wrestle Buroudei down to the ground. Animal snarls and the thud of muscle on muscle and blade on bone crashed through the air. The other alien's knife was stuck in Buroudei's shoulder, and he'd managed to work a second knife up under Buroudei's chin. Buroudei was gripping the blade, blood gushing between his fingers as he pushed upward, but the other alien had the full force of his body weight pressing down. And every second, that blade was inching closer to Buroudei's throat.

I was about to watch Buroudei get slaughtered. And it was all my fault..

No. No no no.

Too much had been taken from me already. But not this. Not him. Not today.

Before I knew what I was even doing, I was up and running, my breath coming in sharp gasps. My vision swam as my legs pumped, and I vaguely remembered the colonel saying something about reduced oxygen in this atmosphere. But still I pressed on. Because there was no other choice.

I had no plan of attack. I just knew I needed to get this other alien off of Buroudei, at least long enough to give him the chance to recover and regain the upper hand. Panic swelled inside me, but I forced it down, sweeping my eye quickly over the situation, trying to grasp at anything that could help. Then it clicked. *His tail.*

There was no time to think my plan through. With a shriek, I grabbed onto the thick, muscled tail of the other alien, pulling with all my might.

It didn't do much. This guy easily had 180lbs on me. But it did enough. The alien jerked back in surprise, and I cried out triumphantly as I saw Buroudei rip the knife from his grip, spinning it and plunging it into his enemy's chest. But the other alien still had some fight left in him, and he gnashed his teeth, swinging his powerful tail and throwing me off of him.

I flew through the air, tumbling into the cargo bay. I smashed into a row of crates, and there was pain everywhere, *everywhere*. I was on my back, unable to move, even as I saw the heavy metal box teetering on the shelf above me. The last thought I had before it fell and threw me into darkness was of Buroudei. And the thought was so vivid that, even as I got ripped down into bloodied unconsciousness, I swore I heard him call my name.

CHAPTER TWENTY
Buroudei

I heard Zeezee's body collide with the hard shell of the fallen thing, and I was filled with such rage that for the first time I saw my enemy's sight stars pulse in fear. He had one knife lodged in his chest and had fallen back, but that was not enough to fell a warrior of the Sea Sands. It did not matter. I would be victorious. I had to be, because that was how I would get to Zeezee. Baring my fangs, I pulled the other warrior's knife from my shoulder, blood pouring. But there was no pain. Only blinding oblivion. The pulse of hungry vengeance pulled to a harrowing point. The need to kill.

He had hurt my Zeezee.

It was time for him to die.

The warrior scrabbled back on the sand, out of weapons.

"Gahn Fallo will know of what you've done. He'll come and take your female, just like he took all the others."

I leaped forward, the knife slicing up through the air to his throat.

"Let him try," I snarled.

With a flick of the blade, I ended him.

I sprang up and ran, back into the fallen thing, to the side of my mate. Fear impaled me when I saw she was not moving. Her head was turned sharply to one side, having been hit by one of the strange square jars. Her beautiful, terrible blood was streaming down her face and dripping from her ears. For the first time in my adult life, or maybe ever, my hands shook from fear. I knelt, bringing them to her perfect, bloodied face. There was the barest hint of breath.

She's alive.

There was no time to waste.

I collected her, as gently as I could, in my arms, bounding out of the fallen creature and leaping up onto my irkdu. My own blood was shockingly dark on her skin. We were too far from the tents, too far from the healers. Clenching my jaw, I realized there was only one choice now.

I cried out, and my irkdu groaned, its many legs working to bring us to the Cliffs of Uruzai.

⟨ ⟩

WE CAME UP ON THE CLIFFS quickly, and I launched off of the irkdu before it had even stopped moving, cradling Zeezee against my chest. I hated her limpness and the blood blooming on her face. The blood coming from her nose and ears was terrifying. I wanted to say so much to her. There was so much she did not yet understand. But all I could choke out were the words, "Do not die."

I sprinted along the cliffs, approaching the entrance to the Lavrika Pools. The Lavrikala there looked at me sharply, drawing her spear, entering into a defensive pose. Without the Lavrika's invitation, there was no reason for me to be there. It was forbidden. But it was the only way.

I did not want to kill the Lavrikala. Such a thing was blasphemy, an atrocity of the highest order. I bit back nausea at the thought that I might have to betray the most sacred ways of our people to save my mate. But I would do it. I knew I would. I just hoped I would not have to.

I skidded to a stop before the Lavrikala, raising my tail before my eyes and dropping to my knees in a show of submission unheard of for a Gahn of the Sea Sands. But I did not care. Not now. Not while Zeezee bled in my arms.

"Gahn, what-" the Lavrikala began, her voice halting in confusion. My tail thrashed back down to the ground, and I saw that she was the same guardian who had been here the night the Lavrika had come to me. I hoped that that was some sort of sign.

"Please, Lavrikala. Please." My voice was a broken growl. "This is my mate. I think that she is dying. You must allow me access to the Lavrikala Pools. She will not live to see my healers."

The Lavrikala was quiet for so long I worried that I would have to kill her after all. But then she spoke, and the relief was like sunlight after a long night.

"I do not believe the Lavrika would want your mate to die out here on the sands. No, this cannot be. Come forward, Gahn. I grant you access to the Pools of Lavrika."

My chest tightened, and I raised my tail once more in a final show of gratitude before I was up, forging forward into the darkness of the cliffs. I pushed through the narrow tunnel, being careful not to knock Zeezee's head or feet against the walls, before I emerged into the cavern with the pools. The Lavrika was nowhere to be seen. It did not guide me in what to do. I had only my own instincts to rely on. With one last look at my mate's lovely face and a final grunt of deep pain, I leaped forward, plunging into the nearest pool.

Zeezee was pulled from my arms at once. As if she were a stone, she sank, while I was buoyed back up. I howled, fighting whatever force was separating us, claws slashing, tail snapping. But it was no use. I was thrown from the pool. I was more prepared for this than last time, and I landed in a crouch before sprinting back to the pool and attempting to re-enter. But I was thrown back as soon as my skin made contact with the surface. An agonized roar tore from my chest. I could not get to Zeezee. I could not help her. I should have never brought her here at all. The pain was unlike any I had ever known.

I had doomed her.

And I had doomed myself.

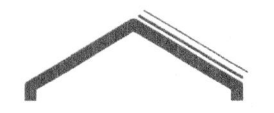

CHAPTER TWENTY-ONE
Cece

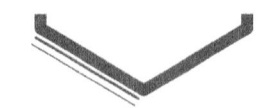

Everything was white. All glowy and soft and cushiony. I floated freely, no clue where I was, blinking, dazed in the face of all that white. There was something familiar about it, but I couldn't put my finger on it. It was like something from a forgotten dream. I shook my head back and forth slowly, trying to figure it out before giving up. I wasn't warm, and I wasn't cold. I didn't feel hungry or tired or in pain. To be honest, I didn't feel much of anything at all.

Maybe I died. Don't they talk about a white light when you die?

The thought didn't bring me any real emotion. I felt like I was wrapped in gauze, everything held back, on the other side, away from me. But there was something wrong with the idea that I'd died. A tiny, niggling pain that I became aware of slowly. The feeling that I had left something important behind.

I blinked again, and suddenly there was a face before me. It was white, too, and glowing. I had no idea if it had been there the whole time or if it had just appeared. For a split second, I thought it was my Grammy, and then I was pretty sure that, yup, I'd died. But another blink brought the face into better focus. It wasn't Grammy. It wasn't human at all. It was huge, something between a snake and a dragon, with gigantic, knowing eyes. It opened its massive mouth, revealing three rows of wicked teeth and a tongue forked into three parts. That image stirred something deep inside my brain. *Three tongues...*

Buroudei.

I gasped. Or I would have, if I had been breathing. I wasn't sure if I was floating in gas or liquid or some element that I didn't even know existed. Whatever. It didn't matter. All that mattered was that I didn't keep going into whatever this light was. Because I had to get back to Buroudei. I had to make sure he was OK. He'd been fighting. And he'd been hurt.

"Please," I said, and my voice echoed as if from everywhere. "Please, help me go back." I didn't know what this creature was or if it would help me, but it was the only thing here and it was my only fucking shot. The dragon head opened its mouth wider. Then the long ribbon of its body, legless and wingless and invisible until that moment, wound around me, squeezing. "Please," I begged. I couldn't stay here. Not without him.

I didn't know if the dragon creature could even hear me. My whole body was wrapped up in its glowing form. The only part of me still exposed was my head. The dragon's mouth got bigger and bigger, bigger than should have been possible.

It reared forward, taking my head into its jaws.

And bit down.

《 》

"YOU MUST LIVE, ZEEZEE. You must. I cannot think without you. I cannot breathe. If you die, I will wander the sands forever bereft without you. I will let the zeelk strip the flesh from my bones, and even that will not be enough to atone. That pain would be nothing to this. You must live. You must fight. You must. *You must.*"

What was that? Was this the dragon talking to me? Was I inside its mouth or what? I groaned, opening my eyes. My vision swam, but right away I could tell I was somewhere different. For one thing, there was stuff to see besides endless glowing white. Dimly lit stone walls and a high, rounded ceiling. And a set of huge, dark eyes with glimmering metallic specks pulsing in the centre.

"Buroudei," I whispered. I felt my face split into the biggest fucking smile. I couldn't help it. I was so glad to be back here. To be with him. "Am I ever happy to see you."

Buroudei froze. The specks in his eyes exploded and swirled, and he brought his face closer. I felt his hands on either side of my jaw, and wanted to nuzzle into them.

"How is it you can speak to me?"

His voice was deep, gruff, and perfectly understandable.

Um. What?

"Excuse me? Hold on. Rewind."

Buroudei's face darkened and he hissed.

"A moment ago I heard you speak. I understood you. But now I do not understand what you say at all. What is 'rewind?'"

Holy fucking shit. I sat up, gasping, and Buroudei jerked in surprised.

"Lay back, my mate! You were injured very badly."

I squeezed my eyes shut, thoughts tearing through my mind, as Burdouei's hands ran all over me, from scalp to toes, checking for injuries. My brain was moving about a thousand miles a minute. I could understand Buroudei. And he could understand me. And he'd called me his mate... Which, just... What?

"OK, one thing at a time." I opened my eyes to find Buroudei's face an inch from mine. I gulped. "How can we understand each other?"

I could tell that I wasn't speaking English. I was speaking his language, but as easily as if it were my own native tongue.

Buroudei sat back on his haunches now that he was satisfied I wasn't injured. He stared at me.

"I do not know," he said slowly. "I brought you to the Lavrika Pools for healing. This must be a gift from the Lavrika."

"What's a Lavrika? Oh. You mean that dragon thing?"

He frowned.

"I do not know this word."

Dragon had come out in English, like *rewind* had earlier.

"This big long white animal. With a huge head and eyes."

Buroudei took a sharp breath.

"Yes. That is the Lavrika. The spirit of this place. You saw it?"

I nodded eagerly.

"Yes, I think so. It wrapped itself all around me, then tried to eat my head. I guess. Or maybe not."

Buroudei's tail thudded.

"I do not understand this. But I will not question it. Being able to speak with you is a treasure I could not have fathomed. I did not think I would ever get to talk to my mate."

"That's the second time you've said that. Why do you keep calling me that?"

His jaw clenched, and for a moment he looked crushed, but he composed himself quickly.

"The Lavrika allows warriors a vision of their mate and it awakens the sacred mate bond between them. Many days ago, I was summoned here to see my mate. And I saw you in the pools." His face softened. "And then, some days after that, I found you. And my life has been bathed in glory ever since."

I flushed. *Damn.* Had he been saying stuff like this to me the whole time? I might not have fought his advances off so much if I'd known that I was bathing his life in glory. If a human guy had such a thing to me, I would have laughed my ass off. But when Buroudei said it, it didn't sound over the top. It just sounded sincere and true. Plus, the fact he was gorgeous and hulking and brooding helped. My eyes trailed over his face, his neck, his shoulders -

"Oh my God, wait, your shoulder! That guy with the knife. He got you! Are you OK?"

I sat back up and crawled over to him, my hands brushing across his skin and finding no sign of the battle.

Buroudei caught my hands in his, drawing them to his chest.

"The Lavrika's blood healed me as well as you."

I glanced over at the shining body of liquid next to me. It looked like the same glowing milky stuff Rika used at the healers' tent. *I guess Buroudei and I both took a little bath.* I didn't seem wet, though. It definitely wasn't a normal liquid.

Relief coursed through me as I turned my eyes back to Buroudei, and I couldn't hold back the flood of emotions that came with it. My throat tightened, and tears burned in my eyes.

"When I was alone in there, in all that white, all I could think about was getting back to you."

The admission made me feel raw and vulnerable, but I wanted to be vulnerable with Buroudei. Because I knew that he would keep me safe.

He groaned, capturing my face with his strong hands, then crashed his mouth against mine. I opened immediately against the onslaught, tears streaming more freely now. Buroudei pulled back when he felt the wetness on my cheeks and dabbed at them curiously.

"What does this mean, this wetness from your eyes?"

I laughed, rubbing the back of my hands across my eyes quickly.

"I guess it's a human thing. It happens when we're sad."

Buroudei looked horrified, and I rushed to explain.

"Or happy! Or relieved. Or stressed. Or if there's a physical injury. Basically when anything intense or overwhelming happens, someone might cry."

Buroudei looked as if he were thinking hard.

"To cry... This is a *human* thing. Human is the name of your tribe?"

"I guess you could say that." Even with my newly acquired language skills, I still wasn't sure how to explain how I'd gotten here. But Buroudei seemed satisfied for the moment.

"Human or not, you are now a woman of the Sea Sands. Once we are mated, you will be crowned the Gahnala of our tribe. And together we will rule our territory and have many cubs."

Somehow I had more questions now that I could understand Buroudei than I had had before. Mated? What did that mean? Like, going all the way? What was a Gahnala? And many cubs? Like, kids? Little half-human, half-kangaroo gladiator babies?

I sighed, pressing my thumb and forefinger to the bridge of my nose and pinching.

"I feel like we have a lot to talk about," I muttered.

Buroudei stood and held his hand out for me, the human gesture that now looked so natural on him. Without hesitation, I took it, warmth spreading through my whole body. He looked happier than I'd ever seen him. And despite all the weirdness of this moment, it was beautiful to see.

"Come, my mate. We have time. The journey home is long."

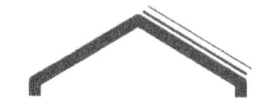

CHAPTER TWENTY-TWO
Buroudei

The Lavrika was a truly generous being. It had brought me the perfect mate, it had saved her life, and had now given us the gift of a shared tongue. I could not have imagined the joy I felt when Zeezee spoke and I understood her for the first time. Her beautiful voice was no longer a tremulous, nonsensical song in my ears. I could start to understand her precious thoughts. And I could have her understand mine.

I wrapped my arm tighter around her as we journeyed home over the sands on the irkdu. The night air was full of her questions, but I did not mind. I would spend every moment of the rest of my life answering her questions, if it pleased her. I had questions of my own, but they could wait until her curiosity was satisfied.

"So, explain this mate thing to me again?"

I bent and smiled against her hair. *With pleasure.*

"Mating is when a cock and a cunt join in great pleasure to create a cub." I hardened at the thought, my flesh aching at her back.

"No, *God,* I know that. I mean, tell me more about how mates get chosen and what that means."

I frowned, ignoring the fact I did not know the word God, and tried to explain.

"It is much as I have said. Warriors are called by the Lavrika to see their mate. This awakens the sacred mate bond between them, which means they now live their lives for each other. It is like awakening to the reason for your existence." I smiled as I remembered the first time I saw Zeezee. *A glorious explosion of destiny.*

"So only warriors get called to see their mate? And that automatically makes the woman in love with him?"

"I do not know what *in love* with means."

She sighed, bringing her delicate fingers to her chin and rubbing.

"It means that you love them more deeply than anyone or anything else. That you want to spend your whole life with them. Maybe it's more complicated than that, but that's the gist of it. At least for me."

This was familiar to me.

"Yes, the sacred mate bond is like being *in love*." I fought disappointment as I realized what her question meant. That she did not feel the sacred mate bond awaken the way I had. "You ask when the mate bond awakens in the woman. It should awaken the moment the warrior sees her face in the pools." I paused, trying to ignore the band of pain tightening around my chest. "Does this mean that it did not awaken in you? You are not *in love* with me?"

She grew still, her back stiffening. Her voice was quiet when she spoke next.

"I didn't say that."

I did not know what to make of that.

"Based on what you said, I am *in love* with you. I feel that I must be the most *in love* of any warrior who has ever lived. How does a human warrior make his woman be *in love*?" Whatever it was, I would do it.

Zeezee groaned.

"You really have a way with words, you know that? And you can't make someone be in love. Humans don't work that way. We fall in love. For some people it happens quickly, for some it takes more time."

"But *how* does it happen?" I could not keep the growl of irritation out of my voice. All this talk of falling and time was making me impatient. I wished to understand immediately so that I could make Zeezee be in love with me right now.

"Nobody knows. It's different for everyone."

I tried not to be dismayed.

"But how is it for you?"

She laughed softly.

"I don't really know, to be honest. I guess it kind of happens in stages. You meet someone, then you start to like them, then you like them a whole lot, then maybe if all goes well you fall in love with them. But then again there's also love at first sight, so who knows..."

The mating rituals of the humans made no sense to me. But my perfect mate was human, and I would learn her ways.

"Where do I fall in these stages?"

She stiffened again, her words coming haltingly.

"Um, well, I definitely would say that... I like you a whole lot."

Satisfaction snapped in me like a cord pulled taut. Pride surged, and I held my weapon a little higher with my free hand.

"This is good," I grunted. "For you I am only one step away from *in love*, then. I am very close."

"Well, it's not that simple," she said, sputtering. I ignored her words, grinning as I looked out over her head. She could not take away the fire of hope blazing in my chest, now. Zeezee liked me *a whole lot*.

Zeezee grew quiet, and I took the opportunity to ask some of the questions that had lived inside me these past days.

"Where is the human tribe? I saw you come down with the fallen thing with some of your people. Where are the rest?"

"Ah. It's a bit difficult to explain." Her hand rose, pointing up at the night sky. "That *fallen thing* is something we call space ship. It helps us travel, but it's not alive. It's not like your irkdu. We come from up there. From another planet. We flew here in the space ship."

"What is a planet?"

"Like... another world. Out there. Beyond the stars."

It could not be. How was such a thing possible?

"So you do not come from Zaphrinax?" I had never heard of such a thing. I did not know anything existed beyond our lands.

"Is Zaphrinax the name of this planet? Or, this world, this place? No, my people live on another world called Earth. Way out there." She pointed up again then paused, and I heard the smile in her voice when she spoke next. "But I think there are some humans here. On Zaphrinax. I didn't see the bodies of my friends at the wreckage. I think they may be alive."

Confusion nipped at me. Did Zeezee not know her people were with Gahn Fallo? Perhaps in the chaos she had not seen. Her hair had been flying everywhere and blocking even my own vision, after all.

"Yes. I believe they are still alive. They were taken by Gahn Fallo."

She jerked around in her saddle, her eyes wide and her gaze hard.

"Wait. You know what happened to them? You know where they are?"

"Yes. I saw Gahn Fallo's men kill the zeelk and collect the other women."

Her smile was like sunlight.

"That's amazing! Well, we have to go get them!"

She turned around to face forward again, squinting over the desert lands, as if she could find them that way. I bent, and spoke against her hair.

"We will. Gahn Irokai is bringing his men to ally with us. We will do battle with Gahn Fallo and retrieve your people."

For some reason Zeezee did not seem happy with this.

"Battle... I'm not so sure I like the sound of that. Can't we just go talk to them?"

I grunted.

"That is not the way of the Sea Sands. And Gahn Fallo is a vicious warrior."

Zeezee sighed. The tents of our tribe were coming into view.

"Well, I guess I'll just have to accept that, for now. I definitely don't want the other women with a bad guy, so we'll have to do what we have to do. So he's a Gahn, like you? A leader?"

My mouth tensed as I thought of Gahn Fallo. He was a strong warrior, and brave, but he was treacherous. He was the only current Gahn of the Sea Sands who had taken his position by killing his own tribe's previous Gahn.

"Yes. There are five mighty Gahns of the Sea Sands, leading the five tribes. Gahn Fallo's territory is closest."

We passed the boulders, and I jumped down from the irkdu, turning to help Zeezee to the ground.

"Fighting it is, then. But no getting stabbed this time, alright?"

I lowered my lips to the top of her sweet head.

"I will do my best. For you."

She turned her face up towards me, her soft lips parted.

"Thank you, Buroudei. Really. For everything. For looking out for me, for taking me back to get my stuff, and for agreeing to help get my friends back. I can't wait to see them."

I wanted to tell her it was all for her, that I'd do anything for her, but even though that was true it was not the whole truth. I stroked my knuckles across her cheek, and watched with interest as a flush moved under her skin.

"I am happy to do it. And it is good for the tribe, too. We do not have many women, now. My men are eager to fight for your friends."

Her gaze narrowed with suspicion and she jerked back, knocking my hand away.

"Hold on. You don't have a bunch of other guys in your tribe thinking my friends are their mates, do you? This needs to be a no-strings-attached rescue! I don't want them thinking that by helping bring my friends back they get some wife out of the deal."

"Only the Lavrika can show a man his mate. And so far, it has not come to any other men in this tribe." This, too, was not exactly the whole truth. But I decided not to tell her about Taliok. Not yet.

"Hmm. Alright. I guess that's good enough."

I helped Zeezee untie some of her belongings, carrying them to my tent. Some of the larger things were left with the irkdu as it grazed. We would get them tomorrow. For now, all I wanted was to be among my hides with my mate. To touch her. To taste her. To see what being liked *a whole lot* truly meant.

CHAPTER TWENTY-THREE
Cece

I tossed the backpack I'd salvaged from the ship to the ground beside the bed of hides, sinking down with a groan. It had been one hell of a long night. It felt like we'd left on this journey days ago. I was feeling stiff from the long ride back here, and I rubbed my thighs absentmindedly, thinking back over everything Buroudei had said. Being able to talk to him was kind of mind-blowing. After all the frustration and miming, I could finally just ask him what I wanted to know. And there was still so much I wanted to know.

Buroudei came into the tent after me and dropped the clothes and items he held before lighting a valok candle. When he saw me rubbing my legs his face grew dark. He stalked towards me, ripping my hands away and probing at my legs.

"Hey, cut it out!"

His strong touch was a ticklish torture along my stiff muscles. My body jerked in response. But he ignored me, quickly pulling the pants right off me.

"Buroudei, come on! Hey, now that you can understand me, I can tell you to knock it off!"

I had no underwear, and I pulled my tunic down, trying to cover my crotch and legs. But Buroudei was stronger. He wrenched my legs apart with hands that were impossibly firm and gentle at the same time. But he did not move after that. He knelt between my legs, studying my skin closely, before running a single knuckle from the inside of my left knee up to my groin. His touch sent electric sparks zinging under my skin and heat flooding into my cheeks. Then his tail twitched, and he sat back on his heels, looking satisfied. I eyed him warily.

"What? What were you looking at?"

He cocked his head, as if the answer should have been obvious.

"The leg coverings worked."

I blinked, then glanced at my pants, the pants that Buroudei had reinforced with strong leather.

"Oh, yeah," I said, almost disappointed that that was all he was looking for. "I thought you were going to... you know... *mate* me."

Buroudei's nostrils flared, and his fists clenched on his knees.

"It is all I long for in this world. But I needed to make sure you were not injured from the long journey." His brow contracted moodily. "And, I could understand you saying, 'no.'"

I was kind of regretting telling him to knock it off now. It had been a bit of a reflex to say no, but as he squatted, watching me with an intensity I'd literally never seen in another man's eyes, his loincloth straining, I couldn't deny that I wanted him. I had started wanting him even before tonight. But then again, that was before I knew all about this sacred-mate, make-babies-with-me stuff.

I decided to stall.

"Why do you think the Lavrika told you I was your mate?"

Buroudei's answer was instant.

"Clearly because you are perfect. And you are the perfect mate for me."

Damn. What did I say about this guy having a way with words? If he keeps throwing stuff like that at me, I'll be mounting him myself.

I shook my head quickly, my messy braid flopping back and forth.

"No, I mean, why a human? Why are there so few women around here?"

He settled himself on the sand, sitting cross-legged, and sighed.

"That is the fault of my foolish ancestors."

I inched closer to him, getting more comfortable. His eyes tracked my every movement.

"Go on. What happened?" I wanted to know more about his people, his history. And just why oh why I of all people had ended up as his *sacred mate*.

He sighed again.

"It is a long history, but I will do my best to make it short. The Lavrika helps us keep the balance of our people. It is deeply tied to every part of us and this land. This is why its blood can heal. And why, I think, it was able to give you our language."

I nodded slowly. I was mostly following. I mean, as much as an Earth girl could follow a story about a magical snake-dragon that helped aliens get it on with each other.

"It is imperative that we follow the visions of the Lavrika when choosing a mate." He gave me a meaningful look, and I cleared my throat, suddenly very interested in how my nails looked. Spoiler alert: not great.

"The men of the Sea Sands can only father cubs of one kind. Either boys or girls. It does not matter how many cubs a man sires, they will all be either male or female. Some generations ago, women started rejecting their mates after realizing their mates would produce girl cubs. Many women wanted to be the mother of a Gahn, and they sought new partners to have sons."

"Wow. You guys put men above women that much?" I couldn't help the judgmental tone of my voice. Buroudei's tail lashed powerfully, his voice hardening.

"A warrior treasures his mate above all else and would never reject her. As I have said, it was the women making these decisions. And those decisions were honoured and respected. Until we started to understand the repercussions."

Oh. So it wasn't as simple as *boys are better than girls*. The women had a lot of power and agency, too. I thought of Rika and Balia, how respected they seemed among the tribe, and nodded, waiting for Buroudei to continue.

"We did not know how important it was to follow the Lavrika's visions. Though it is possible to produce children outside of a sacred mate bond, it is very difficult. Our birth rates fell, and of the cubs who were born, most of them were male. Within three generations, we were brought close to the brink of extinction. And this happened in every tribe of the Sea Sands. It was only by returning to the Lavrika's ways that we have been able to start to rebuild. Though it is slow. Until you arrived with your other women, we thought we may never truly recover."

The weight of his revelations clanged like a gong inside my head. Me being Buroudei's mate wasn't just about him wanting me. It represented something much more important than that – the survival of his people. The balance of the whole planet.

No pressure.

"You said it was the women choosing to leave their mates before. What about now? What if a woman rejects her mate now?" With men outnumbering women three-to-one, it seemed like the women should have their pick of options.

"It is extremely rare for such things to happen now. We have seen the devastation this can cause. Besides, like I said before, the women of the Sea Sands feel the sacred mate bond, too. They feel, as you say, *in love* with their mates just as much as the warriors do. It is highly unusual now for a woman to reject her mate. I cannot remember the last time such a thing happened in our tribe. It was not within my lifetime." He stopped, grinding his fangs together, then spoke again, but slowly, as if every word pained him. "Ultimately, if a woman were to refuse her mate, she would be allowed to do so, and could go and live the life she wished."

"Interesting," I muttered, chewing my lip. And I had to ask the next question, even though it would hurt him. And maybe hurt me, too. But I had to know where I stood. Was I a captive or not? "What if she's the mate of the Gahn?"

Buroudei's eyes sparked, and suddenly he was on me, pushing me easily to the ground, his hands locked around my wrists, which he raised up above my head. His huge, hard thigh pressed up between my legs, making me gasp, and something else huge and hard pressed against my waist. I arched, my breasts pushed against his muscled chest, my pulse increasing every moment.

I was in trouble now. It was hard to think straight like this. My blood rushed frantically through my body, congregating between my legs, right where his thigh was pressing. He groaned, lowering his mouth. My lips parted involuntarily, and I gave a small moan when he didn't kiss me. Instead he spoke against my mouth, his lips and breath sending shivers exploding down my spine.

"I will not tie you up, my beautiful mate. I will not make you stay here with me. But you should know that, if you flee, I will always follow. No matter where you run, I will find you. I will not force you to live as my mate, but I will always be at your side. Until the very end of my days."

So I wasn't truly a captive. Not really. Buroudei would honour my wishes the best way he knew how. And that was good enough for me. It was the final piece that helped me come to my decision. My decision that I was going to give whatever the hell this was a try. Not even that, I was going to dive right in, headfirst. I already knew that I was falling, and when Buroudei had almost died, and then I had almost died, the only thing I cared about was being with him again. I wasn't going to run. Not from him. Not anymore.

These thoughts were crashing one against the other in my head, and as they did so I was silent, staring into Buroudei's magnetic eyes. But my silence made him uneasy, and his voice came out like broken glass when he spoke next, his hands tightening at my wrists.

"I know I am not of your kind. But am I that displeasing to you?"

Wow. There was a lot there, bound up in those words. Hurt and rejection and insecurity and hope. The fact that this insanely strong, attractive, powerful warlord was insecure over me potentially not loving him was breaking my little human heart. A heart that I was about to wrench up into my mouth and give to him. Because I knew he'd make it whole again.

"Remember when I said I liked you a whole lot?"

He grew very still, and grunted, "Yes."

"Well, I lied. Or, I didn't exactly lie, but I didn't say everything."

Buroudei had turned into stone. It barely seemed like he was breathing. I gulped. *Here we go.*

"I'm in love with you."

Buroudei didn't move.

OK... Slightly anticlimactic.

"The sacred mate bond! I feel it for you. I'm saying I want to do this... Be your mate."

The words were embarrassing, and I started wiggling under him, looking off to the side, face on fire.

"You could say something, you know," I whispered, anxiety pulling at me. Buroudei sucked in a great breath.

"Forgive me, Zeezee. You have broken open my world and put it back together again. Your words have forged futures I never thought I'd live to see. It is difficult to speak."

"I know what you mean." I turned my head back to look into his eyes. The glimmering, spaced out shards of his eyes were practically vibrating. He gave one maddeningly slow thrust against my abdomen and my core tightened with need. I nodded feverishly, and Buroudei groaned, taking my mouth in a wet, heated kiss before trailing that amazing tongue down over my neck to run along my collarbones. He let go of my wrists, yanking my tunic up and over my head, and I was naked, totally bared to him. And it was more exhilarating than anything I'd ever experienced before. Buroudei knelt, running his hands over my sensitive breasts, then down over my waist and hips before reaching my thighs once more. I could feel the wetness growing between my legs as he parted my thighs, staring at my spread pussy.

"You really must be from another world." His voice was husky and low. "Because there is nothing here so beautiful as you. So beautiful it becomes a kind of pain."

I stared at him, breath shuddering in and out of my body, every part of me clenching and aching with need.

"Pain?" I breathed.

Buroudei slipped the pad of a finger against my soaking folds, and I moaned, bucking my hips upward.

"Yes. You are so beautiful it hurts."

Oh, God. What the hell was a girl even supposed to say to that?

Buroudei stroked his finger over me, slowly, exploring every part. When he brushed my clitoris I cried out, and tried to grind against his hand.

"Your cunt is beautiful. It is so wet for me. And so soft." One more long stroke almost had me coming undone. "It goes against every instinct, but I want to blunt my claws, just so I can feel you more."

Oh, right. That's why he was being so slow and careful. I was already forgetting how different we were.

"Don't," I choked out, even as my body screamed for him to touch me more, touch me *now*. "You're perfect." I didn't want him to change a thing. He was my perfect alien warrior. My mate. I almost laughed at the thought, and chided myself for drinking the alien Koolaid. But I didn't care anymore. All I cared about was him and this moment and the building waves of need, deep inside. My legs were shaking, my breath coming in little gasps. I was about to sit up and beg this gorgeous alien to fuck me, but I didn't need to.

With a broken growl, he descended, burying his face between my legs.

The way Buroudei went down on me, like my body was slaking a terrible, lifelong thirst, was almost more arousing than the actual physical sensations. And the physical sensations were pretty damn good. The longest, centre part of his tongue circled my aching entrance, while the outer parts slicked up and down, brushing my clit teasingly with each pass. It wasn't long before I was clutching at his head, grinding my hips, pressing myself harder against his face. I'd never been this free of inhibitions when a human guy had been down there before, and sometimes I got so self-conscious I couldn't even come. But this, with Buroudei? The alien who was worshiping my pussy like it was saving his fucking life? Yeah. It was pretty easy to let go and just *feel*.

The waves were growing bigger and bigger. Coming hotter and harder. Buroudei didn't let up for a moment. And when that centre part of his tongue entered me, thrusting in and out, his fingers tightening like iron at my thighs, I came. I came and came, until I felt as crystallized and shattered as the shards in Buroudei's eyes. And still he did not stop, until I was pushing against his head with my hands, pulling at his ears, crying out in sensitized agony.

He rose, his face tense with need, my wetness on his mouth and chin shining in the flickering light of the candle. Fuck. That was an image that would be burned into my brain forever. The image of my huge warrior, every muscle pulled tight with longing, right before he took me for the first time.

My mouth went dry, and I rose up on my elbows, spreading my legs wider. His eyes roamed over every part of my exposed form. As he took me in, he removed every leather strap from his body, yanking the knives from his back. Then, with a quick, fluid movement, he removed his loincloth, and I sucked in a breath at the sight of him.

Even on his knees he towered, a wall of alien muscle, his cock like thick, dark stone. I reached a hand towards it, but he gripped my wrist, grunting. He didn't need to say a word for me to understand that he was already close to coming. The thought inflamed me, and I clenched in anticipation, lying back.

Buroudei moved over me, his expression ravenous, and I felt his hardness settle between my legs. Even though my blood was running hot, his skin felt hotter. He dragged his tip experimentally along my wetness, up and down. His movements were precise, almost stiff. As if he were trying not to lose all control. But I kind of wanted to see what he looked like when he lost control. I arched my hips up, pressing my wet entrance against his tip, and he shuddered before plunging inside.

He was huge, and there was a moment of heat as I stretched for him. But I was so wet, so ready, that before I knew it all I could feel was the overwhelming pleasure of being so filled with him. Buroudei made an inhuman sound against my ear as he pulled back and thrusted once more. I whimpered as the two flexible but firm spears of flesh alongside his cock got pressed upward under Buroudei's weight, rubbing against my clit. Every time he pulled out, that pressure on my clit lessened, And when he plunged back in, the pressure surged to an Earth-shattering, or should I say Zaphrinax-shattering, point.

He was going slowly, still holding back, trying not to hurt me. But there was no pain. Only the need for him to drive in faster, harder. My hands scrabbled against his muscled back, nails scratching as I breathlessly bucked against him, urging him with my body.

Despite our differences, despite the fact that we weren't the same species and came from different corners of the sprawling universe, he understood me perfectly in that moment. He rose up and back on his knees, pulling my legs up. He was so big that my legs didn't quite reach to comfortably go over his shoulders, my ankles instead landing just above his pecs. He gripped the front of my thighs against his torso, breathing harshly, bending and running his nose along my foot and down the inside of my calf. He nipped at the side of my knee, and I cried out, tightening around his cock. He groaned, his dark eyes meeting mine, and I felt him pulse inside me in response. Then he straightened again, and guided my legs to fall and spread.

Hell yes. I locked my ankles around his back, barely able to reach, as he planted his hands on either side of my torso and began thrusting, slow and firm at first, then harder and faster. It was overwhelming in the best possible way. Like my entire body, entire being, was filled with him. There was something so animal and primal in how I responded to him, wanting him to rut me harder. Wanting him to claim me. His tail thrashed on the sand as his movements grew erratic. I reached up, gripping his elbows, needing something to hold on to. Otherwise I thought I might get shot out somewhere into the galaxy with the force of the hot pulses building inside me. Those spears were crushed against my clit, rubbing in the most maddening way as Buroudei hammered into me.

His gaze seemed somehow both hard and unfocused as his eyes bored into me, lips drawn back, fangs bared. I didn't turn away, didn't close my eyes. I wanted to see all of him when he came. The thought of him coming, brought to that brink of pleasure because of my body, pushed me over the edge, and I screamed, everything tightening around him as my orgasm tore through me. I'm pretty sure I slipped into English, or maybe even gibberish, as words I didn't even know I was saying tumbled out of my mouth.

Buroudei kept on thrusting through my pleasure, driving me to the edge of insanity. He lowered himself onto one elbow, moving his free hand up to grip my breast. His breath was hot against my throat, and when I felt the touch of his fangs, in my ecstasy I almost wanted him to bite down as hard as he could. But he didn't, instead snarling against my skin as I moved my hands down his back to his ass, feeling the way his powerful glutes clenched as he drove into me. Just when I thought I couldn't take it anymore, that the sensations would completely overthrow me, I felt every muscle in Buroudei bristle then clench. Then his head reared back and he roared, so powerfully that it sent reverberations through his body and mine. I felt that roar, deep in my pussy as he came, pulsing and spurting inside me. He gave a few more thrusts, wringing the pleasure out, and I just held tight to him. Because that was all I could do. My body was reacting based on pure instinct now, my lizard brain taking over. And it wanted to hold on fucking *tight*. As if to keep Buroudei at my side. To keep him *inside*.

    To keep him with me. Forever.

CHAPTER TWENTY-FOUR
Buroudei

This was it. The reason for my existence. The purpose driving my entire life. The answer to every question I had ever had. Being with my mate, nestled in her soft body, was a pleasure so exquisite it almost did not seem real. And yet, it made everything more real. Every sensation was magnified, every sense sharpened. The scent of Zeezee's arousal, the slick tightness of her cunt, the smooth milk of her skin – all of it was making and remaking me. I felt truly a Gahn, now. Built into a better sort of man. Because of Zeezee.

I was already stirring with desire again, even though I'd just spent myself so forcefully into Zeezee's warmth. But we both needed to rest after our long journey and the trials we had endured tonight. And we had more trials ahead: the battle with Gahn Fallo. Regretfully, I pulled out of her, and she gave a wordless mew of disappointment. That one sound almost undid my will right then. I growled, low in my throat, laying down then pulling and turning her so that her back was against me. My half-hard cock was pressed beautifully between her thighs.

"This doesn't feel close enough," she complained, wiggling her rump, pressing against my cock. I gritted my fangs, bending my head to whisper in her hair.

"You must rest, my mate."

"Don't need to..." She said, even as her words trailed off in a tiny, adorable yawn. I pulled the dakrival hide up over the both of us and nuzzled closer, breathing deep the intoxicating scents coming from her hair and neck.

"Mmm." She grabbed at the arm I'd slung over her torso, snuggling up to it. Curse me, she was irresistible. My cock pulsed. But I could already feel her drifting into sleep. I tried to quell the burning of my blood, taking long, slow breaths. Zeezee's breath came rhythmically, a haunting melody to punctuate my dreams.

She had fallen asleep. I forced myself to relax and do the same. Because wherever Zeezee went, I would always follow.

《 》

ZEEZEE WAS STILL ASLEEP when I awoke the next morning to the sounds of new voices, shouts, and many irkdu. My blood rushed through me and I rose immediately, strapping my loincloth and weapons on with practiced ease. I was not expecting Gahn Irokai and his men to have gotten back this soon. But if it was not him, it would have to be Gahn Fallo. Black rage rose in me at the thought of Gahn Fallo threatening me here, among my tribe, where my precious mate slept. I would slay him on the spot for the insolence.

"Buroudei?" Zeezee was rising, sitting and rubbing her eyes sleepily, and the sight, though soft and lovely, pierced me like a spear. She was too beautiful for this world. I longed to dive back into the hides with her, to see what she tasted like when stained with sleep. But there was no time.

"I hear warriors. I must go. Stay here."

Her eyes grew huge, her face turning white. I could not stand around and explain. I gave her a hard look, as if to reinforce my command that she not move. The last time I had told her to stay in a tent, she had not listened. But she could understand me now. Somehow, I was still worried she would not listen.

With one last, long look at her, I turned and jogged out of the tent, heading towards the sounds. About forty irkdu were approaching the tents, and my warriors were already gathering, weapons drawn. Galok sprinted to my side, squinting, then giving a wild cry.

"Gahn Irokai has returned!"

He was right. At the head of the pack of irkdu was a beast carrying Gahn Irokai. I grinned, raising my axe in greeting as they approached. They had made very good time. Such good time I would not have believed it. This was fortuitous. We could put our plan into motion even quicker than I'd anticipated. Then we would have all the human women, and Zeezee's gratitude would forever drench my cock. My blood surged at the thought of the battle, and of claiming Zeezee afterwards, again and again. I was sure I looked half-crazed as I smiled widely at Gahn Irokai, who had dismounted and was stalking towards me, followed closely by Taliok.

He stopped before me, and we raised our tails. Taliok and Galok did the same.

"You have made very good time, Gahn Irokai."

His tail thumped. Taliok's gaze was intense upon me.

"My men were willing to push themselves beyond anything before. This cause is a noble one. I will not deny that many of my men hope for a mate from among the new women."

I stiffened, some of my excitement abating. I'd ignored the fact that we hadn't addressed what would happen after the battle with Gahn Fallo. I was not willing to let Gahn Irokai take all the women. My Zeezee would not be happy to be separated from them again.

"Has the Lavrika come to any other men in your tribe yet?" I asked, my gaze narrowing. Gahn Irokai watched me closely, then slashed his hand through the air.

"No. Only to Taliok."

This was good. So far, we had equal claims to the women. I had a mate from among them, and so did one man from Gahn Irokai's tribe.

I wondered if, after battling Gahn Fallo, Gahn Irokai would turn on us, and try to take them all for himself. Clearly, he was thinking the same thing about me as his gaze bored into me. Wondering if I would betray him.

I was not sure what would happen. I knew that Zeezee wanted to be reunited with her friends, and that I would do anything to make her happy. And if that meant fighting with two Gahns, then, so be it. But for now, Gahn Irokai was my ally. I needed him, just as much as he needed me.

To dispel the tension in the air, I smiled, relaxing my stance.

"We are glad to have you here as allies. Come, set up your tents. You will need rest after your journey. We will leave at dawn tomorrow."

"This is acceptable," Gahn Irokai grunted. Then he and Taliok turned to relay their orders to the other warriors. With Gahn Irokai's numbers, our forces were more than doubled. We had more men than Gahn Fallo, now. Yes, I was sure we would be victorious. This would work.

《 》

GAHN IROKAI AND HIS men spent much of the day sleeping in the tents they'd brought. They truly must have ridden almost endlessly to get here so quickly. But with the potential of finding a fated mate driving their desires, I could not blame them. I did not get to spend any time with Zeezee that day. Galok and I joined the hunters. With so many extra mouths to feed, we would need to bring down more dakrival than usual. We were lucky to find a large herd, though, and killed eight of the great horned beasts, dragging them back behind our irkdu. The women and children got to work skinning and butchering the animals, and by the time Gahn Irokai and his men emerged, the sun was dipping, and the evening fire was blazing, meat sizzling on huge bone skewers.

I stood, raising my tail to Gahn Irokai, gesturing that he and Taliok to join me at the fire. They and their men approached warily, but soon enough everyone had settled in and was eating. Gahn Irokai sat on my right hand side, Taliok to his right. Galok was seated on my left, but he leaped up, raising his tail to his eyes and moving, when Zeezee appeared with Rika for the evening meal. My heart was a clenched fist in my chest. Though it had only been one day, I ached for her already.

Rika sat with Balia on the other side of the fire, and Zeezee looked between the healers and me, as if unsure. She was likely unsure if she should be next to me when I was conversing with another Gahn. But no Gahn's presence would keep my mate from my side. With a quick word to Gahn Irokai, I rose, jogging to her and taking her hand.

"Hello," she said, and even in the dimming light I could see the crimson smear of desire across her cheeks. If I slipped a claw beneath her tunic and sniffed, I knew I'd smell her arousal, too. But there would be time for that later. Her small hand safe in mine, I led her around the fire, returning to my place next to Gahn Irokai. My hackles rose as I felt the eyes of many warriors fall upon her, some with apprehension, some with curiosity, many with lust. If any man looked too long, I'd be forced to tear his eyes from his skull.

Galok, who was now seated on Zeezee's left, having moved over for her, seemed to sense the dark waves rolling off of me. He averted his eyes and took a large bite of meat, chewing forcefully, staring into the flames. Taliok, however, did not avert his eyes. His tight gaze tracked back and forth between Zeezee and me, forcing a warning thrum to build in my throat. Only then did he finally look away, though the gesture did not seem submissive.

Gahn Irokai distracted me from my possessive rage by speaking.

"Have you learned anything else about these women? About where they come from, who they are?"

"They come from a place we have never known. Beyond the stars."

Gahn Irokai sucked in a breath.

"Impossible," he said, regarding me with suspicion.

"Trust me, I know how you feel. But it's true." Zeezee's voice drifted past me to Gahn Irokai, shocking him like lightning from a desert storm.

"She speaks!" He thundered, rearing back. Taliok jerked to look at us, jaw tight, sight stars spinning.

"Do you deceive me, Buroudei? Last time she pretended she could not speak."

I was about to answer when Zeezee cut me off. I was not used to having a woman speak for me like this, especially to another Gahn. But Zeezee did not seem like she could be stopped. She shook her head quickly, leaning around me to better see the other Gahn.

"No, it's true. I couldn't speak your language then."

"Then how do you speak with us now? You only have one tongue. It does not seem like you would learn our language so easily."

My pride flared in defensive anger. How dare he insult my mate's perfect, single tongue.

"Zeezee has learned many of our words on her own. Her people are resourceful and intelligent."

Zeezee patted my shoulder.

"It's OK. He's right. I'm good with languages, but I'd never learn to speak it this fast."

Between the two of us, we pieced together the story of our night at the *space ship*, including how I'd killed one of Gahn Fallo's men, and how I'd rushed to the Lavrika Pools to heal Zeezee. Gahn Irokai looked drawn. Taliok was silent.

"I wonder if am I grown too old to be a Gahn, in times like these. Strange things are afoot."

I snorted, knowing Gahn Irokai was not serious. No Gahn would ever admit to a true vulnerability like that, not in front of another tribe's men. He was one of the most powerful warriors of the Sea Sands, even at his age. I imagined it would be many ages before he would choose a successor, or call for a baklok, a tournament meant to determine a tribe's next Gahn if there was no successor chosen.

Gahn Irokai and Taliok did not continue the conversation, lost in their own thoughts. I turned my attention to my mate as Balia laid down a bone tray with the choicest bits of meat before us, raising her tail before returning to her seat. Zeezee grinned, reaching forward and to grab some meat and popped it in her mouth.

"Mmm. Tastes like steak." I did not know what *steak* was, but the eroticism of the image before me led me to think it was something to do with mating. I pulled her against my side, sniffing at her neck, at that sweet spot behind her ear as she gasped, then giggled.

"Hey, I'm trying to eat here!"

It was good she was eating. Though the Lavrika Pools had healed her completely, she had still been through a lot. Lots of food and good rest were in order, especially since she would soon be carrying our cub. The thought lit a fire in my chest, and my arm clenched around her, my cock growing hard. I could not wait to mate her again tonight.

After eating, we bid goodnight to our allies, and Zeezee and I returned to our tent. As soon as we were inside we were on each other, mouths searching, hands grappling. As I reached for the hem of Zeezee's tunic, to pull it up and over her head, she stopped me, yanking it back down.

"Wait, wait a second. Before we get down and dirty, we should talk about tomorrow."

I frowned.

"What is there to talk about?"

"Well, like, what's the plan? I know we leave at dawn. But is there anything else I need to know?"

Perhaps the Lavrika had imparted our language imperfectly. I thought I had heard Zeezee say "we."

"The other warriors and I," I began carefully, watching her with suspicion, "will leave at dawn tomorrow. Gahn Fallo's territory is one day's ride from here. We will attack tomorrow night and retrieve your people."

She crossed her arms, causing her breasts to plump up in the most delicious way. I reached for her again, but she stepped back.

"Doesn't sound like a complete plan to me. You left something out. Or someone."

"And what, or who, is that?" I asked dryly. I already knew the answer.

"Me. I'm coming with you."

CHAPTER TWENTY-FIVE
Cece

Buroudei didn't seem to like that I wanted to come with him. His face hardened, and he stared at me flatly as I told him I was coming with him. But what the hell did he expect? That I would just let him ride off into the sunset with his warriors, tossing women over their shoulders like cavemen? I ignored the fact that that was exactly what he'd done with me.

"You are not coming."

I rolled my eyes.

"And why is that? Because I'm a woman?"

Buroudei cocked his head, as if confused by a question with an obvious answer.

"Yes."

My mouth fell open. I wasn't expecting such a blunt answer, but I shut it quickly.

"Where I come from there are male and female warriors, you know!"

Buroudei looked thoughtful for a moment.

"Are you one of them?"

I felt heat creep up my neck. Ah, yes, Officer Celia Heaney, a well-trained, decorated soldier in the regiment of the Department of Linguistics at the University of Toronto. Good grief.

"No," I admitted. "But I'm still coming."

Buroudei sighed, reaching forward to brush a finger along my lower lip. I fought the urge to open my mouth and suck. *I need to be serious here.*

"It is too dangerous, my mate. You do not know how to use a blade. If you are present, I would only be distracted."

A sharp pang went through me as I remembered how terrible my distraction had been last time Buroudei had been fighting with another warrior. It had almost cost him his life. But, then again, I'd still ended up helping him in the end.

"I don't plan on fighting. I'll stay far back, and wait until everything is over. Maybe there won't even be any fighting. Can't you just creep in and sneak my friends out?"

"That will not be possible. And it is not our way. We settle things on the battlefield, not sneaking under the secret cover of night."

I blew out a harsh breath.

"I don't understand why you need to kill each other over stuff like this, especially when your population is so depleted. Alright, well, battle or not, I am coming. I haven't seen my friends in days. I need to make sure they're alright. I *need* to, Buroudei."

My throat tightened with unexpected tears. I was desperate to make sure my friends were OK. If I could have gone to see them tonight somehow, I would have. Now that I knew they hadn't died that first day, I couldn't wait to see them face to face. And beyond that, I needed some human connection. Something to tie me to my old life, just a little. I loved Buroudei, and I was happy to be with him. But I needed to be around my people, too.

Buroudei's mouth flattened as he thought about my words. I got the sense I was wearing him down. I pressed on, laying argument upon argument, feeling like I was a lawyer arguing my case before a very attractive, very grumpy tyrant of a judge.

"I'm the only one who speaks both languages. What are you going to do, storm in, kill Gahn Fallo, and take my friends by force? They'll think you're abducting them. They'll think you're worse than Gahn Fallo. They won't want to go with you. Some of them may even get hurt. You need me there so that they can talk to me and see that it's safe to come with us." He didn't respond, instead sitting down cross-legged on the hides. I knelt in front of him, placing my hands on his knees, leaning in. My nipples hardened through my tunic as they brushed against his chest. I felt him stiffen, but still he did not speak. He eyed me warily.

I moved up and forward, straddling him, pressing my butt against his straining erection. As if he couldn't help himself, his hands ran up the outside of my thighs, gripping my hips. One of his thumbs moved inward, drawing circles over my clit. My pulse skyrocketed, and I tried not to grind against his touch. Instead I wiggled myself on his cock, watching as he swallowed hard, every muscle in his neck straining.

I moved my hands from his shoulders to the sides of his rock-hard jaw, bringing my face in closer until we were nose to nose, speaking against his mouth.

"Please, Buroudei. My mate. My Gahn. This is something I need to do."

Apparently calling Buroudei *my mate* and *my Gahn* was equivalent to breaking out the big guns. He groaned, his hands clenching at my hips, before he forced my mouth open with his tongues, his thumb working faster against my clit. I was already so close.

"Let me come," I whimpered, pulling back from the kiss. I almost laughed when I realized the double meaning in my words.

"You have no honour in your negotiations," he muttered darkly, voice gruff. His hips rocked, his cock pressing against me as his thumb circled. Pulses of pleasure were building, now. Just as I was reaching the edge of orgasm, Buroudei stopped, looking me in the eye. I held my breath in anticipation.

"I will bring you with us. But you will remain with Galok on his irkdu, far from the battle. That way you can speak to your friends immediately after our victory. And if we are not successful, he can bring you safely back."

I could have cried. I threw my arms around his neck, and kissed him, over and over, mumbling, "Thank you, thank you," against his lips. He groaned, and moved to lay me down, but I stopped him, pressing gently against his chest, indicating that he should lie down instead. I was already so wet as he laid back, watching me. I stripped my tunic away quickly, then undid his loin cloth, his hardness straining straight upward like some incredible alien stone formation. He hissed as I ran my fingers up and down. I wanted to be the one giving him pleasure right now. He had done so much for me, and was going to put his life on the line for me and my friends tomorrow. He was so good, and all I wanted in this moment was to be good to him. To show him how much I wanted him, and how much he meant to me.

I moved forward, placing myself above his hips, rubbing my wet folds along his tip as I worked my clit with my fingers. Buroudei looked luridly fascinated, his breath becoming ragged, his nostrils flaring. His hips bucked up against my wetness, and with a small cry, I pressed myself down onto him.

Seeing my big, bad alien flat on his back for me like this was fucking intoxicating. I waited a moment, allowing myself to adjust to his girth, then started moving up and down, up and down, over that hardness. I alternated touching myself with caressing the two spears of flesh beside his cock, urging them against my folds to crest at my clit. *Fuck me.* I was going to come already.

Buroudei didn't look like he would last much longer, either. His hands ran up my sides, brushing over my breasts then squeezing, the muscles in his thighs and glutes clenching as he rocked up into me. Unable to take it anymore, I leaned forward, placing my hands flat on his chest and lifting my hips a little so that he could drive into me harder and faster. His hands moved down to grip my ass, hard, massaging the flesh there as he hammered upwards, his movements becoming erratic and primal. One of his hands slid up my back to my neck, pulling me down until my torso was flat against his as he thrusted. His fingers buried themselves in my hair, and his breath was hot against the side of my face as he groaned.

"Zeezee, my mate, I... I am undone by you."

For a species our military had described as primitive, that was a hell of a lot more poetic than anything I could manage at the moment. All I was capable of saying as I came was, "Oh, fuck, fuck!" My voice became strangled, words fading into a keening whine as Buroudei gave a few more powerful thrusts before exploding inside me.

I collapsed into him, all my muscles giving out at once. I pressed my face into his broad chest, reveling in the solid strength of him. A knot of nerves took root deep in my guts as I thought about tomorrow. About the fact that something could happen to him. But there was no other way to get my friends back, and I wasn't willing to leave them in the hands of a Gahn like the one Buroudei had described.

With a slick pop, Buroudei shifted, pulling out, leaving a clenching emptiness inside. He ran a large hand up and down my back as I laid on top of him.

"I would mate you again and again tonight, Zeezee, if I had my way. But we must sleep. Dawn comes on swift legs."

I nodded into his chest, sliding down until I was nestled into his side. He pulled the hides over us, and chewing my lip, thinking of tomorrow, I fell into a restless sleep.

《 》

BUROUDEI KISSED ME awake before dawn. In my sleepiness, all I wanted to do was melt into that kiss. I snaked my arms around his neck, pressing myself closer. I felt him harden against me, and his kiss grew deeper, before he pulled back with a growl of complaint.

"We must prepare ourselves, my mate."

Right. Today was the day. Adrenaline jolted me awake, and I got up, quickly yanking on my tunic and my new riding pants. I scrunched my sun protection jacket up and shoved it into the backpack, along with a couple of water bottles, before slinging the bag over my shoulder and putting on my socks and boots. Then I combed my hair with my fingers, tangled from sleep, sweat, and sex, and tied it into a messy braid.

As I got ready, Buroudei dressed in his usual loincloth, adjusting his erection to get it on. Then he layered strap after leather strap across his chest and back and hips, tucking many ablik blades of varying sizes against his skin. I couldn't help but stop and stare. There was something distinctly masculine and erotic about the way his muscles rippled and bulged as he carefully strapped his weapons into place. He hefted his axe, tucking it into the usual place at his belt, and grabbed the spear he'd retrieved from outside the space ship, turning to face me.

I pressed my lips together, my heart pounding. Standing at his full height with his spear at his side, he looked awesome, and not awesome in the *wow-that's-so-cool way,* but in the *holy-fucking-shit* way. He inspired awe. And a lot more than that. He inspired love.

I rushed towards him, enveloping him in a hug.

He dropped his spear, arms circling me. I felt his hand brush at my braid, fingering the loose hair at the end.

"I am very glad you have fallen *in love* with me, Zeezee," he said against my hair. I let out a small, tearful laugh, pulling away and swiping at my eyes.

"Yeah, you and me both." It was strange. But it was true.

And with that, we were ready. We exited the tent and moved to join the others.

Buroudei's warriors, as well as those of Gahn Irokai, were already hard at work getting everything ready out by the boulders beyond the tent. A massive herd of irkdu, ours and theirs, remained still as their masters loaded them with weapons and supplies for the journey. I watched as women brought valok and dried meat, carefully wrapped for the trip, to the men packing the irkdu. When I saw Rika speaking to another warrior, I turned to Buroudei.

"How come you don't bring Lavrika's blood to a battle? That way you can heal people who get hurt."

Buroudei led me towards his irkdu. It was easy to spot. It was the only one with the saddle. As he began detaching my saddle, he answered my question.

"To heal fatal wounds, you need large amounts of Lavrika's blood combined with the skills of a healer. Unless you go to the Lavrika Pools, as we did, but that is not common practice. It was the first time it has been done, to my knowledge."

My heart swelled as I digested this fact. No one had ever gone to the pools to get healed before? And Buroudei had done that, just for me?

I cleared my throat.

"OK, but can't you still bring some small jars anyway, just in case?"

Buroudei pulled the saddle from his mount. Though it was a large piece of equipment, it almost looked like a toy in his arms.

"It is pointless. The Lavrika's blood does not stay fresh long in the sun. It must be kept shaded, so it is difficult to travel with. When our healers travel to the pools to refresh their supplies, they must take special heavy jars and travel with canopies over their irkdu to keep it fresh before reaching the shade of their tents where they store it deep in the sand. It is not practical to bring all of that to battle, especially when, without a trained healer, we would only be able to deal with very superficial wounds. And we do not bring our healers to battle as they are too important to the tribe." He stared at me as he said that last part, and I panicked, thinking he might suddenly change his mind about bringing me with him.

"OK, I get it. Let's go find Galok." I spoke quickly as if to distract him. He regarded me warily, but acquiesced all the same. He left his spear resting against his irkdu's side, hefting my saddle and taking my backpack from me.

"I can carry it. It's my stuff."

Buroudei just grunted. He did not give it back.

It didn't take long to find Galok. Even with the addition of Gahn Irokai's men he was still the tallest of the group. His long black hair, usually flowing freely down his back, was braided for battle.

"Galok. Your orders have changed. You are to travel with Zeezee on your irkdu, and keep her out of harm's way. You are to keep her away from the battle, and only if we are successful in our endeavor, are you to reunite with the group."

Galok's brows contracted.

"You mean I will not be fighting? I will not be joining in the glorious battle for the new women?"

"Hey," I cut in, not sure I liked the way he'd phrased that. I didn't like the idea that my friends were being fought over like objects.

Buroudei's voice lowered in warning.

"Galok. These are your orders." Then, his voice softening somewhat, Buroudei added, "There is no one else I trust to do this for me."

That seemed to satisfy Galok for the moment, and he raised his tail over his eyes. I was beginning to recognize the gesture as one of greeting, acknowledgment, and respect.

Buroudei handed the saddle to Galok, then turned to caress my cheek.

"I must go speak to Gahn Irokai and ready my mount."

I nodded, leaning into his touch.

"I understand. I'm good here."

His tail twitched. Then, with a quick, soft kiss on the top of my head, and a *don't-fuck-up* look tossed at Galok, he put down my bag and moved away through the crowd. I watched him until I could no longer see him among the other men, and then turned to Galok.

Galok was strapping my saddle to his irkdu with ease, as if he already knew how. It struck me as strange, since I hadn't seen a single other person use a saddle.

"You really seem to know what you're doing," I remarked as he got everything into place. When he was finished, he turned to me.

"Yes. We use saddles when we are cubs."

I frowned, unsure if that was meant to be some kind of backhanded comment. But Galok grinned, and I relaxed. I didn't know him well, but Buroudei trusted him, and so far he seemed like a pretty good guy.

"Do you have any children?" I asked. His face fell for a moment, then blanked into expressionlessness.

"The Lavrika has not yet blessed me with a mate. But soon, I hope. Very soon."

Poor guy. It was heart breaking to see how lonely these warriors were. But the amount of hope so many of them seemed to be placing upon the human women was making me uncomfortable. I was pretty sure that not all of the other girls would be as happy to fall into bed with an alien as I apparently was. I changed the subject.

"Sorry you got stuck with babysitting duty."

He cocked his head.

"I do not know this word, *babysitting*."

"Ah, I mean, sorry you have to look after me instead of joining in with the other men."

He grabbed my bag and handed it to me before helping me up into the saddle. Then he got up behind me, making sure there was a good few inches of space between our bodies. I stifled a laugh at the subtle show of chivalry. Or maybe, rather than chivalry, it was done out of fear of what Buroudei would do to him if he got too close.

"Do not concern yourself. It is a great honour to guard the Gahnala."

Gahnala. That was a word I hadn't had the chance to ask Buroudei about in detail yet.

"What is that? The Gahnala."

I strained in my saddle to look at Galok behind me. His gaze was unnaturally intense on my face and he leaned forward, the glimmers of his eyes drawing tight. Then he shook himself and shifted back a few inches further. *I guess I'm just as alien to them as they are to me. Not like he's ever seen a human woman this close.* His obvious curiosity didn't offend me. In fact, it was kind of cute. If anyone else ended up with a willing human mate, I secretly hoped it would be him.

"The Gahnala is the mighty Gahn's mate. She is very respected among our people. Usually, after a Gahn is mated with his woman, there is a ceremony to mark her as the Gahnala. But there has not been time for that yet."

A ceremony? Like... a wedding? I flushed at the thought and turned around, facing forward.

"Thanks."

We didn't get much more of a chance to speak after that. Because soon after, just as the asteroid moons were falling and the hot Zaphrinax sun began to rise, we departed, and the sounds of the irkdu and the battle cries of the warriors would have swept my voice away, unheard, over the sands.

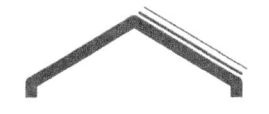

CHAPTER TWENTY-SIX
Buroudei

Gahn Fallo's territory was beyond the Cliffs of Uruzai, a full day's ride from our tents. We maintained a good pace over the sands and did not stop for breaks, eating and drinking as we rode. Anyone who needed to stop to relieve themselves did so quickly, before speeding up to rejoin the group. I rode at the head with Gahn Irokai and Taliok. Normally Galok would also be at my side, but he was in the middle of the pack with Zeezee. By staying in the middle, she would be shielded from any potential predators or threats that could accost us. So far, there was no evidence of zeelk or krixel activity. And that was very good.

As we passed the Cliffs of Uruzai, I muttered an excuse to Gahn Irokai and fell back, slowing until my irkdu trawled along next to Galok's. Zeezee smiled at me, her face shaded by the hood of her human cloak. Her skin was bluish-white, like it had been the first time I'd seen her, and she had strange black shells over her eyes that I had never seen before. She must have seen me looking because she took them off, waved them around, then slapped them back on her face.

"They're called sunglasses. They protect my eyes from the sun."

I stab of dismay went through me. The sun didn't just hurt her skin, but also her eyes? How truly fragile was my pretty mate?

"Do you need to stop and rest?" I asked, suddenly worried. It wasn't in the plan to stop, but I could convince Gahn Irokai to do so if needed. But Zeezee shook her head.

"No, I'm OK. I'm sure I'll be stiff, but this saddle is great, and I've got water and snacks and everything." Her tone grew hard, then. "I want to get there as soon as possible. I want to get my friends."

Pride replaced my dismay. My little warrior, willing to go to such lengths for her people. I urged my irkdu closer to Galok's, and reached for her. She reached, too, our hands brushing momentarily across the distance. Though it was difficult, I tore myself away and returned to the front with Gahn Irokai.

"You brought your mate?" He grunted, not looking at me. But I felt Taliok's gaze upon me as I spoke.

"Yes. She is the only one who knows both languages and she can speak to the other females for us." I paused then, sighing. "She insisted."

Gahn Irokai made a gruff, amused sound.

"So they are like our women in at least one way, then."

I cast him a questioning look, and his lined face broke into a small smile.

"Stubborn."

I thought I noticed Taliok urge his mount to go a little faster.

It did not take long before we officially entered Gahn Fallo's territory. We all became more tense, our gazes constantly tracking the horizon. Each tribe had vast areas of land, and it was impossible to patrol the whole area daily. But there was still the chance of being seen by a patrol or hunting party. I held my axe in one hand, my spear in the other. The landscape changed as we moved further, the sweeping desert becoming more hilly, rindla flowers, thorny axrekal berry shrubs, valok plants, and peet grass dotting the ground. Beyond these hills, where the flat ground met a great sheer wall of rock, were the tents of Gahn Fallo's tribe. We would be there soon. The sun was already beginning its descent, lining the world with shadows.

We snaked through the hills, our pack forced into a thin line in places. Eventually we cleared the hills, reaching the flat plain that butted up against the cliff where Gahn Fallo made his home. In the rapidly dimming light, I could just make out the tiny shapes of tents along the rock face.

I slowed, once again drawing back to reach Galok's irkdu. This is where I would leave Zeezee. She would be somewhat sheltered in the hills we'd just passed through.

"It is time," I said, bringing my irkdu to a stop. Galok did the same, and the other warriors went around us.

Zeezee nodded gravely, pushing back her hood and taking off her *sunglasses* now that it grew dark.

"Be careful," she whispered, her eyes shining.

I had planned not to do this. I had planned to break from her easily, without too many words or touches. The things that would make this harder.

But when I saw her sweet face, the tremble of her lips, I could not help myself. I bent across the space between us, gripping her about the waist and yanking her over to my mount. Her rump landed directly between my thighs as she faced me, her legs draped over mine.

Our mouths met like the thunderheads of a rare Sea Sands storm. Hard and explosive. I gripped her hips as her hands found their way to my jaw, and she arched against me. She muttered little words between the crashing of our lips, words like "I love you so much," and, "Don't get hurt."

I wanted to give her everything, promise her everything. But I could not promise her that. This battle would be bloody, I had no doubt.

I would have stayed there all night had I not heard the warning shouts coming from the group that had moved away from us. Galok stiffened, and I immediately hoisted Zeezee up and over, dropping her into his arms. He helped get her settled back into her saddle as she looked around wildly.

"What's happening? Buroudei, wait!"

But there was no time to wait. A patrolling party had spotted us, and Gahn Fallo's forces were heading this way even now. Galok clicked his tongues, turning his irkdu sharply, and they sped away through the hills. As they moved away, the last thing I saw was Zeezee's terribly pale face as she turned and leaned around Galok, looking back.

Now was not the time for pain of the heart. Now was the time to fight. Fight, and be victorious, so that I could see that small, pale face again.

With a savage roar, I turned my mount and raced towards the battle.

I caught up with our group quickly enough. We were plunging forward over the plains, trying to get to Gahn Fallo before he and his men were fully prepared. But that did not quite happen. Before we reached their tents, the tents that likely housed Zeezee's people even now, irkdu began moving towards us from the crags in the cliff face. Battle cries rang out from both sides, and in moments, our forces met in a Zaphrinax-shattering crash.

I dodged the deadly launch of a spear, howling, bending and urging my irkdu to move even faster. I would take out any man. I'd take out a thousand men if I had to. I would do this for Zeezee and her friends.

All around me, men and irkdu fought. One warrior came my way, blade in hand, ready to be thrown. I ducked just in time, hefting my spear up as he leaped from his mount onto mine. As he landed, I drove my spear into his guts, then yanked it back, letting him fall to the ground. Another warrior came for me, and another, but I made short work of them. The triumph of battle rushed through me, a song in my blood, as I hacked through the crowd. In the fray, from the corner of my eye, I saw Gahn Fallo and Gahn Irokai on the ground, locked in vicious combat. A snarl ripped from my throat as Gahn Fallo bested Gahn Irokai, sinking his blade into Gahn Irokai's chest. I started moving toward them, and saw Taliok was doing the same. But Gahn Fallo was quicker than the both of us and quicker than the injured Gahn Irokai. He plunged a second blade into Gahn Irokai's guts, then slashed, spilling blood and organs to the sand.

Though Gahn Irokai was not of my tribe, he was my ally in this fight, and the sight provoked a brutal rage. I cried out, urging my irkdu faster, faster, until I was almost upon Gahn Fallo. I pulled my axe from my belt and threw my spear as I leaped from my mount.

Gahn Fallo watched me jump, pulling a blade from his back as he dodged my spear. His laughter split the air.

And then I was upon him.

CHAPTER TWENTY-SEVEN
Taliok

Gahn Fallo killed my Gahn. Right in front of me. Gahn Irokai, who'd trained me as a warrior, who'd treated me as a son, was butchered, his guts spilling to the sand like the vines of the veroar plants of the mountains. I never roared in battle like other warriors did. The promise to exact vengeance, vengeance like this world had never seen, was a silent one.

I watched Gahn Buroudei leap from his mount in pursuit of Gahn Fallo, and I moved to follow so that I could slay the other Gahn myself when I heard it. Gahn Irokai saying my name.

I jumped to the ground, running then skidding to a halt at Gahn Irokai's side. I knelt. He did not bother trying to stem the flow of black blood from his wounds. Neither did I.

"I do not want a baklok called after my death. I have chosen my successor. It is you, Taliok."

Other warriors may have let grief force them into denial. Other warriors may have told Gahn Irokai no, that he would live to be the Gahn for many ages after this. But I did not. I remained silent as he called out to one of our warriors staggering nearby, clutching at a wound inflicted by the man he'd just slain.

"Oxriel! Witness me. Before I die, I lay the title of Gahn on Taliok."

Oxriel fell to his knees beside me.

"No, mighty Gahn, you will live. We will get you to a healer."

I wanted to strike Oxriel. He was wasting time with his denials. Precious time.

Gahn Irokai groaned, then fixed his unspooling gaze on us.

"Hear me. Taliok will be Gahn. I decree it with my dying breath."

His voice faltered. Black, silent rage seethed inside. Oxriel was fussing at the wound in Gahn Irokai's chest, but I watched the life fade out of his eyes all the same.

"He is dead," I said, rising and scanning the battlefield for Gahn Fallo and Gahn Buroudei. I expected to find them still locked in battle, as both were strong warriors and neither would fall quickly. But they weren't fighting, and I squinted before starting to sprint towards them, trying to make sense of the scene.

Gahn Fallo was on the ground and there was a woman there, too. A woman like Gahn Buroudei's mate. And beyond them, there were more strange women, looking out from between Gahn Fallo's tents.

As I ran, I couldn't help but let my eyes sweep over their faces. I froze, just as I reached Gahn Buroudei.

There she is.

CHAPTER TWENTY-EIGHT
Buroudei

"Surrender the women and you do not have to die."

Gahn Fallo laughed at me, as I knew he would. Surrender was not our way.

He slashed his blade up and in, quickly. I jumped back, but not fast enough, and his blade slashed along my chest, drawing blood. In the heat of battle, I did not feel it. I snarled and pressed forward, swinging my axe, cleaving down onto Gahn Fallo's arm. The blade stuck, deep in the bone, and his knife dropped from that hand. He had another working hand, though, and another blade. My hand shot out, gripping his wrist. I still held the handle of my axe, which kept his one wounded arm immobile, but he channeled all his strength into his other arm, forcing his blade closer and closer to my face. He was slightly taller than I was, with longer limbs, and he was stretching my arms to their limit, which dampened my strength. In a moment of heated frustration, I slammed my head forward, connecting sharply with his jaw. I felt his teeth tear my skin.

The headbutt stunned Gahn Fallo just enough for me to have the time to pull my axe from his forearm and sink it into the meat between his shoulder and his neck. He screamed in anger and fell to his knees. As he fell, he swung the one blade he still held in his working hand at my legs, but I easily jumped over the weapon.

I pulled the longest blade I had from my back, raising it for the final blow. He drew his lips back from his fangs, fangs dark with my blood.

"You will not get a single one of the women. My men will keep fighting you long after I am dead. You will not touch them."

So he will be defiant, even in death. It did not matter. Whether he continued to fight or stopped to beg for his life, he would die, and we would take the women. My hand tightened on my blade and I raised it higher, ready to bring death down upon this fallen Gahn of the Sea Sands.

CHAPTER TWENTY-NINE
Chapman

"Holy shit. I think he went down."

Kat was sticking her buzzed head out from between the tents. Us humans were the only ones outside. The alien women and children had all been smart enough to hunker down in their tents when the fighting had broken out. But us? Nah, we wanted to see what the hell was going on.

"Who?" I asked, leaning around her. I squinted. I was the only one with combat experience among our little group of survivors, but even I didn't have much of a clue of what the fuck was happening.

"It's the big one. The Leader," Melanie replied, her voice flat. I clenched my jaw, following her gaze.

She was right. The biggest alien, the one they called "The Leader" and I called "The Enemy" was on his knees. A new alien, from the group that had attacked, was standing over him, victorious. The Enemy was done for. Even from here, I could see the cartoonishly huge axe sticking out of his neck.

He was gonna die.

And for some reason, that just didn't sit right with me. Maybe it was something about saving the devil I knew. Or maybe it was something else. Without even realizing what I was doing, I started walking out between the tents towards the carnage.

"Dude, what the fuck are you doing?" Kat hissed loudly. I ignored her, moving to a jog, adrenaline cascading through my body, forceful and hot as gunfire.

"Come on," I heard another girl mutter, and then I heard the others start to follow me, jogging behind me in the weirdest rag-tag group you could ever hope to see. The other girls stopped at the edge of the tents, but I kept going, breaking into a sprint, my long legs flying. Sweat drenched my back, and my breath came in gasps. The alien I didn't know was raising his blade. He was about to swing -

"Stop!" I screamed, pumping harder. The Enemy jerked his head to look at me from the ground. I was close enough now to see the weird swirly parts of his eyes go crazy.

Fuck you. Don't even try to stop me.

I slipped in the sand, catching myself and snatching a huge knife from one of the straps at The Enemy's back as I scooted around his front, standing between him and the intruder. The new alien reared back, nostrils flaring, his weapon lowering somewhat, as if he were unsure what to do. The Enemy growled something behind me, and I figured I had a sense of what he was saying. Something like *Get the fuck out of my way, human*, or, *Don't bother*. Whatever. This alien had been a royal pain in my ass, but I wasn't about to watch him get slaughtered just so that us humans could hauled off by yet another group of hooligans.

I gripped the huge weapon with both hands, staring murderously up at the intruder. I had always done well with hand-to-hand combat, but I had never gone up against a seven-foot-tall slab of alien muscle. *First time for everything.*

"Bring it on, big boy." I raised a challenging brow.

To be honest, I was bluffing. I didn't stand a fucking chance.

But, by some unbelievable stroke of luck, it seemed to be working.

"Yeah, that's what I thought," I said, jabbing my knife, a knife that was more like a sword in my hands, at the other guy. The Enemy said something else from behind me, and grabbed my ankle. But holy shit, had he ever grown weak, The grip felt almost just like a normal man's.

Almost.

The other alien looked dumbfounded. He stepped back, studying me, then finally turned and called something out into the crowd of fighting aliens. Eventually the brawling slowed and came to a stop, everyone turning to stare at us.

"OK," I said, my bravado starting to slip.

I hadn't exactly thought past this part.

"Now what?"

CHAPTER THIRTY
Cece

"How much longer do you think it will be?" I asked Galok. I was seated backwards in my saddle, staring at him, as if by staring I could make him somehow end the battle. As if I could make him tell me that Buroudei was OK. I wanted to be on the ground. I would be pacing if I were. But Galok wouldn't let me. He said it was for my safety, so that if things went south we could take off immediately. But I had a feeling it was more to do with the fact that he was watching me like I was some kind of flight risk. Like I would take off running after Buroudei the first chance I got.

To be fair, he wasn't that far off.

I was desperate to see Buroudei. To make sure he was OK. To help him, if I could. But instead, I was stuck in some fucked-up staring contest with a very loyal, very *stick-to-the-rules* alien.

Great.

Galok sighed and opened his mouth to tell me, for the umpteenth time, that it would be over when it was over, when we heard the startling call of his name echoing through the dark air. Galok straightened immediately, his ears and tail twitching, looking out over my head. I swiveled in the saddle in time to see one of our warriors, a guy named Malachor, riding his irkdu, fast, really fast, through the hills towards us.

My heart leaped into my throat. This would either mean something very good or something very, very bad.

"Gahn Buroudei requests the immediate presence of the Gahnala," he panted, raising then lowering his tail quickly. Relief melted inside me, warm and sweet.

"He's alive," I said, the words coming out in a soft whoosh.

"Yes. Gahn Buroudei is alive."

Galok gave a victorious whoop behind me.

"So then we have won!"

Malachor didn't seem excited, and something like dread settled in my chest.

"Gahn Fallo is still alive," he said. "But the battle is over. For now."

He stopped speaking to Galok, turning his eyes to me.

"Please, Gahnala, the Gahn requests you right away."

I nodded vigorously.

"Of course. Galok, go, let's go!"

With that, we followed Malachor out of the hills and onto the battlefield.

Only there was no battle. Not being fought right now, anyway. I saw a small number of men who looked to be dead, and others badly wounded, lying on the plain. The rest stood silently, watching in a broad circle, the men we'd come with on one side, and men I did not recognize on the other. We pressed into the circle to see what was happening.

And I tell you, I almost lost my shit. I mean, I knew we were coming here to find the others. But actually seeing one of the humans I'd come with, alive and in the flesh, hit me like a ton of bricks. And it wasn't even a human I liked. It was Chapman, the soldier from the space ship. But in that moment, she looked like a red-headed angel. I laughed and screamed her name, and her head jerked towards me, her eyes widening.

Grinning, I took in the rest of the scene. Buroudei was facing Chapman, and I noticed now that Chapman held a giant alien knife out in front of her. Behind her, slumped over on his hands and knees, was a massive alien I didn't recognize.

Buroudei turned to look at me, and before Galok could stop me, I slid out of my saddle and careened down to the ground clumsily. I sprang back up, running to Buroudei's side. As I collided with him, breathing in his scent, counting every heartbeat to make sure he was OK, I realized that he was bleeding. Black blood coated his chest and abdomen, coming from a long, jagged wound along his upper chest. Fuming, I whirled, staring at the weapon in Chapman's hand.

"You better not have done that," I muttered, and she rolled her eyes.

"I didn't. Relax. And why do you care, anyway? They're aliens."

My gaze flitted from her to the alien behind her. It kind of looked like she was... protecting him?

"You tell me."

Even in the darkness I could see her freckled face grow red.

"That's different."

I was about to tell her that it didn't seem a whole lot different, when I heard the excited shriek of my name. Kat was barreling towards me, followed by Theresa, Melanie, and the other women from the space ship. My face broke into a smile so wide it hurt. They were alive. They were all alive.

Kat reached me first, crashing into me and laughing, followed shortly by Theresa and Melanie, and then the others, until we were all lumped into a massive human hug. Half of us were laughing, half were crying. I was pretty sure I was doing both. The only one who didn't join in was Chapman, who kept her knife raised, her eyes on Buroudei.

"We thought you were dead!" Kat shouted against my ear.

"Same," I replied. "I mean, I thought I was the only one who got away!"

Kat pulled back, tears shining in her huge blue eyes. Her buzz cut had grown out a bit over the last few days, soft, short hairs coming in the palest shade of blonde.

"Nope. All these nutters scooped us right up off the sands and killed all the crab things. Then they brought us here."

"Were they good to you? Were any of you hurt?" I looked from face to human face, searching for signs of mistreatment.

"Don't even get me started," huffed Kat, but Theresa shook her head, cutting in.

"I mean, they didn't roll out the red carpet for us or anythin'. But we're fed and clean. We had a place to sleep. No one hurt us."

That was good to hear.

"Look," I said quickly, pointing back at Buroudei, my poor mate who looked beyond exasperated and confused. "That guy is the leader of the tribe I've been staying with. They've taken good care of me. We're here to rescue you guys."

The others didn't look convinced, eyeing Buroudei warily.

"Honestly, hun, we don't know him or any of those others. We got used to these people, the ones we've been with. You should come back and stay with us. There's more safety in numbers." Theresa sounded concerned.

Uh oh. I hadn't anticipated this.

"I can't," I said, my voice breaking. Kat's invisible brows drew inward immediately.

"Why the fuck not? What did they do to you? Are they using you to coerce us somehow? Why can't you leave?"

"No, no, it's not like that." How the hell was I going to explain all this? That I'd fallen in love with an alien tyrant, the monster behind us now? "It's more like... I don't want to leave."

"You sure hugged him tight when you saw him," Melanie said from beside me, her dark eyes watching closely. Heat raced through me.

"Oh, girl. Oh, no, honey. Tell me you didn't. You didn't have to trade sex for safety, did you?" Theresa's eyes were huge in her pretty, tanned face.

"God, no! OK, this is going to take forever to explain. But I will say right now that that guy, Buroudei, he loves me and thinks I'm his mate. And I agreed to go along with it. Not because I was coerced. Because I wanted to."

"You must have hit your head somewhere along the way," Kat said, wrinkling her nose. Theresa had grown pale under her tan. Melanie remained expressionless. A girl whose name I didn't know piped up from towards the edge of our little huddle.

"Oh, come on, none of you guys have thought about it? They aren't bad looking."

Twenty human voices broke out at once, some professing their own bizarre attractions, other spluttering in horror. Buroudei's growl cut through the noise instantly.

"My mate, would you kindly let me in on the conversation?"

"They don't want to come with us." It hurt me to say it, but I could kind of understand. Even if I didn't have Buroudei, I wouldn't want to leave the tribe I'd been welcomed into. It was the closest thing to home I had on this planet.

Buroudei's tail thrashed.

"They will not come with us?"

The scarred alien who'd come with the other Gahn, Taliok, stepped up next to Buroudei, jaw working, eyes ablaze.

"I refuse to leave my mate with Gahn Fallo's men."

Excuse me? His mate? That was new information. Taliok was staring into our huddle with a look of pained hunger. But I couldn't tell who he was looking at.

Great. One more complication.

"Guys, let's hurry this up. I don't think he's going to last long." Chapman was speaking, looking down at the alien at her feet. He was still on his knees, but now slumped forward on his elbows. I recognized Buroudei's axe sunk deep, in above his shoulder. I swallowed. This was exactly what I'd wanted to avoid. This bloodshed. But this was their culture. And I wasn't going to change generations of their ways by batting my human eyelashes.

I moved out of the huddle, standing next to Buroudei.

"I want to remain with Buroudei. You want to remain with your group. But I don't think we should be separated."

My mind worked, playing scenario after scenario in my head.

"What if," I started slowly, a plan unfurling, "we set up a human camp in a central area. Between all the tribes. So that no one is cut off from anyone else, and all the humans can be together."

Nobody looked impressed with my plan. I repeated it in the alien tongue, and Taliok snarled, and Buroudei's tail thrashed. The other women stepped back, alarmed.

Charming, fellas. Really.

"OK, look, I'm going to be straight with you guys because you need to understand the situation. These people have this alien being, this spirit... I don't know what to call it. It's like a dragon with no arms or legs or wings. Anyway, it summons men and then shows them the face of their future mate. This is, like, soulmate level stuff. It means everything to them. Buroudei saw my face before we ever even got here."

Gasps and looks of confusion met my words, but I kept going.

"I have a feeling that more and more warriors are going to get assigned human mates and are going to want to split us off from the group. There are three alien tribes represented here right now, and there are others out there, maybe looking for some of you even now."

"Well, that's terrifying," somebody said.

"Look, it all seems really weird right now. And it is. But if we want to head this off, and head off future battles like what just happened, we need to come together on this right now. If we all live together in a central location, not tied to any one tribe, we can avoid a lot of bloodshed."

I turned to Buroudei, pleading.

"And you." Then I looked at Taliok, and the other warriors, speaking to them in their language. "If you all agreed to move closer together, to move into neutral territory, you could all be near the humans. And no more blood would have to be spilled over who will take us home."

We had to do this. If we didn't stake out our territory now, and force the tribes to come together for us, we'd be screwed. Just because Buroudei had said women could refuse their mate didn't mean that every alien man out there would feel the same. There were tribes I hadn't even encountered yet, and who knew what they'd be like.

Jeers and complaints ran through the crowd of watching aliens. Buroudei drew me into his side, growling. Taliok turned to the watching men, stepping forward to speak.

"Gahn Irokai is dead. As he died he named me Gahn. It was witnessed by Oxriel."

A warrior nearby thrashed his tail in agreement.

"In my first act as reigning Gahn, I decree that our people will leave the mountains to reside in neutral territory near the new women."

Silence fell. I stared, slack-jawed. Out of everyone, this scarred, moody alien was the last one I would have expected to agree to my idea. Buroudei's arm tightened around my waist.

"I, Gahn Buroudei, I will follow my Gahnala wherever she goes. I decree that we, too, shall stay near them in neutral territory." Then he turned to the alien with the axe in his neck. "What say you, Gahn Fallo?"

"What's he saying?" Chapman asked, her eyes never straying from Buroudei.

"They're agreeing to my idea. They're agreeing to have us all live together in a neutral place, near to all of them. They're saying they'll relocate to live near wherever we are." Chapman pursed her lips, eyes narrowed.

I took a breath, looking down at the injured Gahn Fallo, then added, "I have a feeling it's either he agrees, or he dies."

She spoke immediately. "Tell your boyfriend he agrees."

I swallowed an exclamation of surprise at the way she spoke so easily for the Gahn at her feet. *I wonder what happened while I was gone.*

The other women were starting to nod, muttering about how staying together did sound like the best plan.

"We're all agreed," I said breathlessly, looking up at Buroudei, not really believing that this was happening. That I'd get to be together with my friends, and my mate, without further battles and bloodshed. There were a lot of details that would need to be worked out, of course, and I had a lot more explaining to do to get the humans up to speed. But this could work. This could really work.

"Where will we settle?" Taliok asked. Buroudei thought for a moment, then spoke with decisive authority.

"The Cliffs of Uruzai. They are neutral territory. They cliffs and valleys offer some shelter from predators, and no one will want to shed blood at such a sacred place."

Taliok's tail thumped.

"Then it is done. We will ride back and collect our people. To be clear, our territory will remain ours for hunting, and for any other purposes we see fit. But we will live in the neutral territory to remain near the new women."

"Yes, it will be the same for our tribe."

I relayed this information to Chapman, and she nodded impatiently.

"Yes, yes, that's fine. All good. Are we done here?"

"I guess we are," I said.

Some of the next details were worked out quickly. It was determined that the other women would stay here for now and help prepare for the move down to the Cliffs of Uruzai. I could tell Taliok did not like this.

I spoke to him in the alien language. "Taliok, you won't win over your new mate by forcing her from her people tonight. Let us work this out at our pace, and then see what happens. We'll all be together soon." I still wasn't sure who he'd been staring at. But he seemed to take my words to heart, turning and stalking from us without another word, calling orders to his men as they prepared to leave. They collected their fallen Gahn's body, along with the others, and Buroudei's men did the same. Gahn Fallo was helped to his limp feet by some of his men, dragged towards what I could only assume was their healers' tent. I hugged my friends. Knowing I'd be seeing them again so soon was more than I could have hoped for.

I released the other women, returning to Buroudei's side as he watched Gahn Fallo get pulled away.

"I should tell him I expect that axe back when I see him next," he muttered. I gripped his hand, rolling my eyes.

"Come on. We need to get back. You need to see Rika."

He looked down at the wound on his chest, then smiled broadly.

"My mate, this is nothing for a Gahn."

I hoped he wasn't exaggerating, but I was still anxious. I pulled at his arm.

"Let's go."

We took my saddle from Galok's irkdu and secured it to Buroudei's. It felt so good to settle in and lean back against him. At first I didn't, not wanting to put any weight on his wound, but he'd growled and yanked me to him anyway. When everyone was ready, we began to disperse, heading back the way we'd come.

"You know, your plan helped me tonight," he said as we headed back.

"Oh?"

"Yes. Gahn Irokai and I never agreed upon what would happen after the battle with Gahn Fallo. I worried that, after that battle, I would face another with his men. I knew about Taliok. I knew he would not let the women go with us easily."

I sighed, not able to be really annoyed with him. Not now that he was literally bleeding because he'd been fighting for my friends.

"You should have told me."

I felt his nose against my hair, then neck.

"I know, my mate."

That would have to be good enough for now.

"To be honest, I'm surprised anyone agreed to my idea. You guys are so territorial."

"We are," Buroudei agreed. "And if two of the Gahns present did not have mates from among the human women, I do not believe such an agreement would ever have been reached. But such is the power of a sacred mate bond."

I smiled, unable to help feeling touched by his words. That he felt so strongly for me was incredible. A week ago, I wouldn't have counted myself as lucky. In fact, I would have counted myself as among the unluckiest girls alive. But now? Well, now was a whole different story.

I sighed against Buroudei's chest, settling in for the ride. The desert was wide and the journey would be long. But we were together.

And in that moment, I couldn't have asked for anything more than that.

⟪ ⟫

Thank you so much for reading Alien Tyrant, the first book in the Fated Mates of the Sea Sand Warlords series! I hope you enjoyed reading Cece and Buroudei's story as much as I enjoyed writing it. Book 2, Alien Enemy, tells Chapman and Gahn Fallo's story and it is is available in KU now![1] If you'd like a free bonus (steamy!) scene featuring Cece and Buroudei, please sign up for my newsletter at ursadaxwriting.com/contact[2].

⟪ ⟫

---

1. https://viewbook.at/alienenemy

2. http://ursadaxwriting.com/contact

Alien Enemy

"ARE YOU THE GAHNALA of these women?"

If she were a Gahnala, a queen, then somewhere out there she must have a Gahn. The thought made my lip turn up into a snarl. Any Gahn mated to a woman so disrespectful would be unlucky indeed.

She wriggled in my grip, staring up at me defiantly. My fingers tightened on her cloak.

And then, she was gone.

I jerked back in surprise, yanking hard at what was now an empty cloak. With a groan, I tossed the thing to the sand as the woman crouched then ran. Not only defiant, but devious, too. It was not a becoming combination for a female.

Not that that mattered. Why did I care about such qualities in her? It was nothing to me if she were becoming or not.

She appeared to wear strange shells on her feet, feet that were so unlike mine. She was not built to run in the sands like I was, with my high, strong ankles and long, wide feet. Her legs were short, too, her strides less than half of mine. Despite these shortcomings she ran hard, hard, up the hill beside me, chasing after her fellow women. I watched her for a moment, my curiosity outstripping my need to subdue her. Her face was pulled in a snarl of determination, her arms pumping furiously.

One of her foot-shells caught, and she stumbled, her small hands catching in the thorns of an axrekal berry bush. She did not cry out, simply straightening and starting to run again, though I saw blood streaming from the skin on her hands, and from a line across her cheek where a thorn had snagged. Blood a bright scarlet colour, shocking in its brilliance. I sniffed, hard. I'd already scented the blood of the other women. But this fragrance was hers alone. I breathed deep, committing it to memory, before finally breaking into a run.

I caught up to her in moments, slinging my hands around her waist and tossing her easily over my shoulder. She howled, and fought, but it made no difference. I ignored her attempts to escape, following my men and the irkdu back to the tents of our people.

The walk back was not long, but the whole way the slight weight of her body against my skin was a hot irritation, an itch I could not scratch. It made my cock even harder. And that made me angry.

I was under no illusions about my reputation. I knew people called me the Mad Gahn. But this was the first time I truly felt myself slipping from sanity. She screamed and scratched. I grunted and walked, the whole time trying to escape the word that was frothing in my brain.

Fallo, this is madness.

Madness.

Madness.

Perhaps I was more like my father than I'd thought.

I thought that when I'd killed him, I'd stripped that madness from my blood. But here it was arching inside me, rising to meet this woman's fury. I'd never felt so out of control.

And so brutally alive.

Want more? Read Alien Enemy in KU now![3]

⟨ ⟩

FATED MATES OF THE SEA SAND WARLORDS[4]
BOOK 1 ALIEN TYRANT[5]

"If you should flee, no matter where you run, I will always follow."

Book 2 ALIEN ENEMY[6]

"They call me the Mad Gahn. But I never felt truly mad until I saw her face…"

---

3. https://viewbook.at/alienenemy

4. https://geni.us/ZbCYSM

5. https://geni.us/qWQufS

6. https://viewbook.at/alienenemy

Book 3 ALIEN ORPHAN[7]
"I have trained, battled, and fought my whole life. But winning my mate's love is the greatest challenge I have ever faced..."

Book 4 ALIEN REJECT[8]
"She is a difficult creature, my tiny Kat. But I have never met with a creature I could not tame..."

Book 5 ALIEN EXILE[9]
"Beneath all that makes me strange to you, my heart recognizes yours..."

Book 6 ALIEN HUNTER[10]
"Now that I have found her, I refuse to lose her..."

Book 7 ALIEN VICTOR[11]
"I found her, I saved her, and once I am Gahn, I will claim her. There will be no other tribe left for her but me..."

Book 8 ALIEN SHIELD[12]
"I have always been a patient warrior. But now that I have her in my sights, I cannot wait to claim her..."

Book 9 ALIEN KEEPER[13]
"I will be her keeper, her guardian, her guide. And I will keep her safe no matter the cost..."

---

7. https://viewbook.at/alienorphan
8. https://viewbook.at/alienreject
9. https://geni.us/B7aEp
10. https://mybook.to/AlienHunterUrsaDax
11. https://viewbook.at/AlienVictor
12. https://getbook.at/AlienShield
13. https://viewbook.at/AlienKeeper

Printed in Great Britain
by Amazon